The Dead Man's Medicine

A Bob Ryan Mystery

John Buchak

Printed in the United States of America

ISBN: 9780692312018

For the reason of any type of litigation the following statement has been included in this novel. This novel is a work of fiction. Names, characters, places and incidents either are the product of the author's imagination or are used fictitiously. Any resemblance to actual persons, living or dead, events, or locales is entirely coincidental.

Cover art by Karin Buchak

Photos by www.dreamstime.com

Acknowledgements

To my family and friends who have encouraged me to keep writing my novels and work on getting them published.

To my friend Rick Rofman, thank you for helping me cross my I's and dot my T's. See how much I need your help.

To my daughter Karin, who works so hard designing my book covers and getting all my ducks in a row. Thank you sweetheart I love you more than words can say.

To IWOSC (Independent Writers of Southern California.) Thank you my fellow members for your support.

1

Board….. That's what the conductor, dressed in a uniform that made him look like a doorman at the Plaza Hotel, yelled out trying to get everyone's attention on the train platform. His pastel blue uniform and matching hat only accentuated his rotund round belly that seemed to lead the way as he walked. Head Conductor Stanley Peters was a man not to be trifled with and he made it obvious to all that challenged his authority that he was in control of the train and all its passengers.

Francis Robert Ryan, a retired Los Angeles, California Detective, was returning to his home state of California after living in Florida for five years since his retirement. After visiting his old chief of detectives at his home in Las Cruces, New

Mexico for a few days, Ryan was continuing his trip on the West Coast Flyer heading home. The two old war-horses had spent some time together after Ryan flew in for the visit four days earlier

Being escorted once on the train by a heavy set man in a light blue uniform, Ryan, tired and looking only for a place to sit, paid little attention to the man who had a name tag that read, "Head Conductor Peters."

Tipping the conductor, Ryan entered the large semi-private compartment, to find he would be sharing it with three other passengers. Nodding his head at the men and saying, "Good morning gentlemen," Ryan then placed his carry-on bag next to an empty seat and sat down. One man told him he would be getting off once they arrived in Flagstaff, Arizona. What he didn't know was he would be dead before the train pulled into the station.

All four men seemed to hit it off with conversations about sports, women and even politics, Ryan speaking the least of the group, but listening to most of their bullshit. One man told Ryan that he would getting off the train once they arrived at his destination in Arizona.

The four men talked for hours sharing stories of their professions as three of them slowly worked on a bottle of twelve-year-old scotch. Ryan, who preferred iced tea to any alcohol beverage, gave up social and private drinking several years earlier.

The men seemed professional in all their endeavors that they spoke of and all seemed to know where their careers would be taking them, all but one who had no way of knowing he would die before he reached his destination.

Chris Heschel was a frequent passenger on the West Coast Flyer, traveling from El Paso, Texas to Las Vegas, Nevada, after his monthly visits to his plastic molding company just south of the border in Mexico. Although he could quite easily afford a private stateroom on the train or fly First Class, he enjoyed the company of the other passengers and hated to fly. He also hated very much to drink alone.

Heschel, who appeared to be in his late fifties, was about 6'4". He must have been somewhere just shy of 275 pounds and bald as a cue-ball. Through conversations he revealed that he was divorced twice and had no children. He was void of a driver's license due to several convictions of driving under the influence and was also a very sloppy dresser. The man also loved to hear himself talk. He told the group that once he arrived in Las Vegas he would just call his chauffeur and would have no worries about getting around.

The second man sharing the compartment was John Stafford. He was on his first train ride since he was a kid growing up in Ohio. Most of his attention was devoted to watching the beautiful desert scenery as the train cruised along and though he made many remarks about the beautiful scenery to his fellow passengers, his remarks were seldom acknowledged.

Stafford a well-groomed man around forty-five, stood around 5'8", a svelte 160 pounds, slightly gray hair at the temples, with an otherwise full head of thick dark brown hair. His eyes were a light blue, but because of being very blood shot, they had an eerie look to them. One obvious trait he had was an uncontrollable habit of sweat running off his forehead and down his neck, which he wiped away constantly with a handkerchief.

His very nervous hands made the man appear to be afflicted with something similar to Parkinson's disease and he tried very hard to cover up his shakiness with an occasional joke or quick movements. Though he didn't reveal much about his profession, Stafford after a few drinks let out the fact that he worked in a horticulture genetics lab in Oxnard, California and he was returning from a field lab operation located in the swamplands of Louisiana.

He said as he slurred his words, "The pressures of ma-ma-money hungry maniacs trying to control the wa-world, made my slow trip back necessary."

The third man, a very sickly looking gentleman, introduced himself as Edward Taylor. He spoke softly and said, "Up until my retirement several years ago I was an accomplished engineer with a big name steel-forging mill in Pennsylvania and once my years started to show and my ability to produce quality ideas, I was put out to pasture.

Traveling around the country on the many wonderful trains has become my passion after my dear wife of forty-one years passed away from cancer. The following month in a horrendous auto collision, my two daughters were both killed in the accident."

Stopping to take a sip from his drink and a quick look out the window, the old man continued. "At seventy-seven years old, I have let myself go physically and I don't believe I will see many more sunrises or sunsets."

Although he stood around six foot, Taylor appeared to only weigh around 140 pounds and looked very frail. After a small bout of coughing he said, "I don't have much of a desire to add more years to my ailing body and this current trip that started at Penn Station in New York City will be my last." He spoke of the many beautiful sights he had seen and the way he put it, "Gentlemen, this will most likely be my swan song and it has been a wonderful life up to a point, but I'm past that point."

Ryan noticed that Taylor appeared to be wearing facial make-up but figured it must be for a poor skin condition or possibly for some type of disfigurement. The one thing that did not look right about the man was his clear blue eyes that he tried to cover by squinting a lot and wearing tinted glasses.

2

Ryan, being the only non-drinker in the foursome, watched and listened to the somewhat educated men as they reduced themselves into inebriated bar flies riding on a train. For some reason John Stafford took an interest in Ryan, talking more and more about his employers and asking the question, "What gives them the right to play Gods?"

Ryan told him more than once, "Mr. Stafford, I'm really not interested in your personal life or your work. Please, just let me enjoy a peaceful trip back home to LA."

"But you don't understand Mr. Ryan, people are going to die. "I'm going to die."

"I'm sorry Mr. Stafford, I'm just not interested, its something that does not concern me. My advice to you is to contact the local police department when you get home and speak with a detective who might just be able to help you. My only interest right now is to sit here and read my book and enjoy the remainder of the trip."

After it became obvious to Ryan that the man was not going to leave him in peace, he decided to take a walk to the dinning car and try to get a cup of coffee, and maybe find a quiet place to just sit, read his book and maybe watch the scenery.

Ryan's car was the fourth from the rear of the train so making his way to the bar car was much easier then he thought. Finding a seat he saw was going to be impossible because it was standing room only. From what he could see, in the far left corner stood a small but well stocked bar. The bartender looked like a man who wished he had two more arms and hands to take care of the many customers begging for his services.

In the right corner, propped up and mounted securely to a counter, was a very large coffee pot with a rack of coffee cups and dispensers for cream and sugar right next to it.

Ryan smiled when he saw the coffee pot and headed right for it. Arriving at the same time with the same thought of never-ending coffee was a very well built beautiful woman who appeared to be in her mid forties, a brunette with beautiful green eyes and a pretty smile. When she smiled at Ryan he almost tripped over his own feet as the woman said, "Good morning."

Reaching for the cups, the woman removed two from the rack and said, "I'll hold while you pour."

Ryan placed his book on the table and then his hand on the lever as the woman held the cups in place and filled two to the brim.

Looking at Ryan, the woman asked, "Are you enjoying The Da Vinci Code?"

"To tell you the truth, with all the distractions on this train I haven't had time for much reading or to enjoy anything, until now."

"Well thank you kind sir but what did you expect, you're on the Vegas party train."

"What?"

"I'm only kidding, but it is headed for Las Vegas with a bunch of hopeful gamblers aboard.

By the way, my name is Patricia Gibbs, and you are?"

Reaching for the woman's extended hand Ryan said, "Bob Ryan, nice to meet you Pat."

"How far are you going Bob?"

Ryan smiled and said, "All the way to L.A."

"Great, maybe we can share a little conversation along with the coffee for the remainder of the trip. I'm also headed for L.A."

"First we need a place to sit, Pat, and from the looks of it, that's not going to happen for quite a while."

"There's always the coach seating in number three or four car, towards the front of the train."

Ryan said, "I'm game if you are."

Walking through the ten cars to get to one of the coach cars took only about ten minutes, and on the way Ryan and Pat found out a little more about each other.

While passing by Ryan's compartment, he excused himself and dropped off his book on the seat next to his other belongings.

Only John Stafford and Edward Taylor were in the compartment and both appeared to be sleeping, Chris Heschel was nowhere in sight.

Ryan and Pat continued on their way to the coach car and were very surprised to find that there were very few passengers seated there.

After approximately ten minutes of wonderful brief conversation, Chris Heschel entered the car, saw Ryan and said, "Thank God you're here detective, John Stafford is dead. We need you to come quick."

3

By the time Ryan reached his train compartment, a small crowd had gathered at the doorway. Ed Taylor was blocking the entrance talking with the head conductor Stanley Peters, and they both looked at Ryan as he and Heschel approached.

Taylor said, "Conductor Peters, this is Detective Ryan."

Ryan shook his head and responded, "Retired please, I've been retired many years. Now what happened here?"

Taylor appearing shaken said, "We were both sleeping, when I was startled by John's gagging sounds. When I opened my eyes I saw him pulling at his tie and shirt collar choking out the words, "I can't breathe.""

"Did you try to help him?" Ryan asked.

"I got up and tried to help him, but he just slid to the floor and didn't appear to be breathing any longer."

"Did you try CPR?"

"I checked him for a pulse but he was dead, so I pushed the button for conductor assistance."

"That's it? You didn't try to save his life?"

Shaken by Ryan's comment, Taylor yelled back, "I'm not a damn doctor detective. I didn't know what to do. The man was dead. Do you understand me? He was dead."

Ryan put his hand on the man's shoulder trying to ease the pain he had just caused him and said, "Okay Ed, Its okay, there's nothing you could have done."

Ryan asked the conductor, "Would you know, conductor, if there is a doctor on board the train by any chance? He may have had a massive stroke?"

The conductor told Ryan, "I'll check the passenger list and make an announcement asking if there's a doctor on the train."

Looking at the conductor's name tag, Ryan said, "Mr. Peters don't mention a death. Just that a doctor's assistance is needed and I'll remain in the compartment with Mr. Stafford."

The conductor said, "I'll be right back Detective."

Ryan thought of mentioning it again that he was retired, but then gave it up and entered the compartment.

Being very careful not to move or upset anything in the room, Ryan sat in the seat opposite where John Stafford had been seated. Chris Heschel and Ed Taylor remained just outside the doorway keeping other passengers away.

After studying the compartment for a few minutes, Ryan asked for one of the guys to catch up with the conductor and tell him he needs to contact the police at our next stop.

Taylor asked, "Why? What do you see, detective?"

"Please, one of you just do what I asked, I believe we have something more than a stroke here."

What Ryan noticed while looking at John Stafford's lifeless body lying on the compartment floor, was marks on his collar and red marks around his neck. The dirt appeared to be grease and the red marks looked like he had been strangled. Stafford's hands were clean, almost doctor like clean and well manicured so he died at the hands of someone else.

While Taylor went to get the conductor, Heschel remained behind, but after about fifteen minutes of waiting for the return of the conductor and Taylor, Ryan asked Heschel to go and locate the two men.

As Ryan remained seated he heard someone ask, "What's going on here?"

The man, dressed in a conductor's uniform similar to the first man, asked again, "I said, what's going on here?"

Looking at him, Ryan said, "There's been a death here. Didn't the other conductor let you know?"

Looking puzzled the conductor asked, "What other conductor?"

Responding harshly Ryan said, "The other guy, Stan Peters."

"What are you talking about sir, I'm Stanley Peters. And who may I ask are you?"

Ryan sat back in the seat, looked at the man and said, "First of all, there's been a death here. At first appearance it looked like a heart attack, but after looking at some of the things that just don't look right, I believe it's a homicide."

Mr. Peters said, "Again I'll ask you sir, who are you?"

"I'm a retired Los Angeles homicide detective. My name is Robert Ryan, now where is the other conductor?"

"Look Det. Ryan, the other conductor on this train is Joshua Watts, and there is no way you could confuse him for me. I am Irish and he is

African American and we are the only two conductors on this train."

"Well Mr. Peters, there is a man on this train who is impersonating you, and I think you need to find him before this train makes its next stop. You also need to contact the police at our next stop."

"And why is that sir?"

Ryan stared at him and said, "Because he just might be the murderer of this man, Mr. Peters."

The conductor's mouth fell open as he said "Oh my God."

"So sir, I'll say it again, you need to contact the police, Mr. Peters, and see if there is a doctor on the train?"

"I'll check right away detective."

"Oh and by the way Mr. Peters, where have you been for the past half hour that you haven't checked on things at this end of the train?"

"We had an emergency in one of the forward cars that required my self and Mr. Watts."

"What kind of emergency conductor?"

Whispering softly, the conductor said, "Someone was shooting at the train windows in the forward car and it took both of us to control the passengers."

"Please, a doctor and the police Stanley."

Moving quickly away from the compartment door, the conductor said, "I'll be right back detective."

Just shaking his head while watching the conductor walk away, Ryan said softly to himself.

"That's what the other guy said too."

Standing only a few feet from the compartment doorway, Patricia Gibbs inched closer until she was in view of Ryan, who said, "I bet my coffee is cold by now Pat?"

With a serious expression on her face, she asked, "Are you okay Robert? What happened here?"

"I'm fine Pat. Please don't enter, I'll come out there and explain."

"Ah, is he dead or just passed out?"

"Unfortunately for him, he's deceased."

As Ryan got up and walked out of the room, Patricia asked, "What happened to him?"

"Not sure yet, but it looks like someone helped him to meet his maker."

"Did you know him well?"

"We just met this morning."

"Can I do anything to help?"

"I could sure use that cup of coffee now, and make it a double, black with no sugar please."

16

4

A few miles ahead of the train seated on a dirt embankment, nine-year-old Stephen Tate was on his first fishing outing with his older brother Bill under the Johnson Creek railway crossing. After two hours of moving up and down the creek, they settled in the shade of the train trestle in search of some big cat fish.

Fishing talk was not the topic of conversation. Instead Stephen was excited about the new baseball season starting and his assignment at shortstop on the Grants Township Little League.

Bill, who was only two weeks away from his fifteenth birthday, told his little brother that he was going to have so much fun playing, and having mom and dad watching from the bleachers.

As little Stevie started to answer his big brother, they heard the rumbling of the train, as it got closer to the creek crossing trestle.

Watching as the train slowed down while crossing overhead, the boys whistled, yelled, and screamed, but the noise of the train just drowned out their every noise.

Only a few railroad cars including the double engines that were back to back had passed over, when something large fell from above. It wasn't until it hit the water just twenty feet from the boys that they could see the object was a man's body, bound and gagged.

After all twenty cars had cleared the overpass, and the rumbling noise of the train wheels were disappearing in the distance, the boys who were now standing watched as the lifeless body started floating slowly away from them in the murky water.

Stephen started crying as he hugged his brother and asked, "What's happened Bill? Who did that? Will they come after us? I want to go home."

Bill and Stephen lived about three-quarters of a mile away and other than the Water and Power Plant; there were no other buildings that they could go to for help.

Running along the bank of the creek, Bill and Stevie watched as the body got caught up in some low hanging branches and it appeared to be secure between the bank and a fallen tree.

Leaving all their fishing gear behind, the boys climbed up the steep embankment and started running down the road heading for home.

Charging up the front steps of their house, the boys were both yelling, "Mom, Dad, where are you?"

Mrs. Tate, who was in the garden in the backyard, called to the boys, "Out here boys, what's the matter?"

As they both tried to talk at the same time, their mom said, "Hold on, one at a time."

Looking at each other, Bill said, "Mom, we were fishing under the railroad bridge and as the train went over, a body fell from up above and landed in the water right by us."

Before Mrs. Tate could say a word, Stevie blurted out, "And he was dead mom, the man is dead, all tied up and dead."

"Are you sure boys? It's not a dummy or a mannequin?"

Bill calmly said, "No Mom, It's a man's body, we need to call the police now."

"Billy, your father just left for the market, so let's wait until he gets home, then you can show him before we do something foolish."

"Mom, we can't wait, the person that did this will get away. You have to call the police now."

Reluctantly Mrs. Tate did the proper thing and called the local police department and talked to a Desk Sergeant who said he would send a patrol car down to the creek and check it out.

After telling the boys what the sergeant said, both boys ran out of the front door saying, "We have to meet them there, bye mom."

By the time the boys arrived at the crossing, they saw the patrol car parked with the light flashing and the driver's door open.

The officer was looking over the side of the steep embankment as the boys ran to his side yelling; "You can't see him from here officer. You need to climb down and go under the bridge."

Following the two boys down a path that made the descent much easier, the officer soon saw what appeared to be a body partially trapped under a fallen tree in the creek and quickly called using his cell phone for assistance.

The word spread quickly, and before the County Coroner would arrive at the scene, a crowd of people from the town were hanging off the bridge and standing at the top of the embankment trying to take pictures and just see what was going on below.

It was about an hour from the time the boys first saw the body, until the police removed it from the creek.

The paramedics had declared the obvious- the man was dead before he landed in the creek.

As the report was written down, one of the first things mentioned was, "The victim appears to be a conductor from the train by his a name tag on the uniform."

5

When Conductor Peters returned to the train compartment, he had a gentleman accompanying him that looked like he belonged on a vacation-travel brochure. Wearing Bermuda shorts, a Hawaiian shirt and flip-flop sandals, the man introduced himself as Dr. William Kent and he agreed to examine the patient.

Ryan looked up at the man and said, "Doc, he's a long way from being a patient, more like a statistic at this point and you're at a crime scene so please be careful what you touch."

The Doctor stepped into the room and checked the man for a pulse, looked at the conductor and uttered the words, "This man is dead."

Ryan sat back and said, "Well I guess my work is done here, he is officially dead."

The conductor said, "Detective, we can't leave him here like this."

Ryan coming across a little annoyed said, "Mr. Peters, as a *retired* police detective, the key word being retired, I suggest this compartment be sealed up until the police arrive and myself and the other gentlemen be assigned another compartment."

As Ryan stood and reached for his carry-on bag and book that were on the seat next to where John Stafford had been seated, he noticed that his book had papers stuck in between the pages.

Not wanting to bring any attention to the papers he simply placed the book in his bag and left the compartment leaving the job of sealing it up the room to the conductor.

Chris Heschel who was standing next to the door spoke up and asked, "Can you wait a few minutes while I remove my things and Ed Taylor's things?"

"Where is Ed Taylor?" Ryan asked.

Heschel said, "Last time I saw him he went to get the conductor. Where he went after that I have no idea."

"I never saw or talked to the man." Peters said.

Listening to the two men talk, Ryan Said. "I would be very careful if I were you, Mr. Peters, and leave Ed Taylor to the police to find."

"And why is that Mr. Ryan?"

"Because Ed Taylor is not what he appears to be and may be the killer."

Folding his arms across his chest, the conductor said, "He's a frail old man, who is not in the best of health, from what I remember when he got on the train in Georgia."

Almost simultaneously, Ryan and Heschel said, "Georgia?"

Ryan told the conductor, "Taylor told us that he got on in New York City."

Pulling out a little red book from his vest pocket, the conductor flipped the pages until he got to the car they were standing in, pointed to the compartment number, and then said, "See for yourself Detective, Georgia."

"I predict that Ed Taylor will be very hard to locate," Ryan said sarcastically.

"And where could he disappear to on a moving train Detective?"

"Look, all I'm saying is be careful Mr. Peters, this man could be dangerous."

"Thank you Det. Ryan."

6

Ryan and Chris Heschel removed their personal belongings from the compartment even though Ryan knew it was wrong to remove anything from a crime scene.

Conductor Peters pulled the door closed and used a special key he had on his key ring to lock up the room. The blinds on the windows had all been closed and the body of John Stafford remained on the floor just where it had fallen from the seat.

The Conductor led both men to the next car and pointed to compartment D as they got to it and told Chris Heschel, "There is an opening in this room, Mr. Heschel."

Ryan asked, "Mr. Peters, is it possible for Mr. Heschel and me to be placed in the same compartment?"

"Mr. Ryan, there are not very many compartments we have to choose from."

After looking in his little red book, the conductor said, "We have several passengers leaving the train in Gallup. If you don't mind riding in the Observation Car or the Dining Car until we reach Gallup, I can put both of you in the same compartment, in the next car."

"Oh shit", Ryan said. "You need to have the police waiting at the station in Gallup and only passengers checked out allowed to leave the train, or the killer could be getting off in the confusion."

"I've radioed ahead to the Flagstaff Station in Arizona and they will have a large Investigating team waiting for us. I'm sorry Det. Ryan, but at the time of my call I still thought it was a heart attack, I will call Chief Knight at the Gallup Police Department and request a homicide detective at the station to control and start a homicide investigation."

"Thank you Mr. Peters, I know this is all new to you and you are doing your best."

Continuing to walk towards the front of the train to the Observation car, Ryan asked, "Mr. Peters, is it possible for a passenger to go further forward than the Observation car?"

"Actually there are three cars in front of that one, two baggage cars and an empty passenger car that is being dropped off in Flagstaff."

"Are those other cars locked?"

"Yes, and they only have access from the Observation Car. They *are* accessible from the front of the train."

As they continued to walk forward, Ryan checked the faces on every passenger they passed.

Reaching the car before the Observation Car, they met up with Conductor Joshua Watts. As Mr. Peters explained to Mr. Watts just what the plan was, Ryan continued heading forward in his quest for a seat.

After sitting about forty-five minutes, Ryan stood up and told Chris Heschel, "Chris, I'm going to take a slow walk to the rear of the train and hopefully find that nice young lady that I abandoned back there with coffees in her hands."

"I'll keep an eye on your stuff Detective."

Thinking about saying something, Ryan just smiled and said, "Thanks Chris."

After walking through seven cars, Ryan spotted a woman who was seated in a compartment by herself and he noticed she was wearing sunglasses and a scarf and she seemed very careful not to let her face be seen.

Walking back and forth a few times trying to get her attention, Ryan finally wrote down the compartment letter along with the car number and decided to ask Mr. Peters about her when they spoke again.

Entering the next car he spotted Patricia Gibbs seated in one of the middle rows and sat next to her saying, "I was hoping I would find you."

"I'm sorry, Robert. I just took it as a hint that you wanted me to get lost."

"Not on your life Pat, I was just coming to find you and let you know where we were moved."

"Did you find out who did it?"

"I'm pretty sure it was a man named Ed Taylor, if that's really his name."

"Where is he?"

"He's on this train somewhere, but for now he seems invisible."

"What does he look like?"

"I'm sure he's in disguise now. That reminds me. Have you seen Conductor Peters in the rear of the train?"

"Yes in the Bar Car."

Ryan smiled and said, "Care to join me for a drink?"

"Do you think we might get to finish one before you dash off again?"

"It's possible but no promises. Come on, let's try again."

With only two more cars to walk through, they were at the door to the Bar Car in less then a couple minutes, even with Ryan stopping several times and checking out passengers by tapping on their door windows.

The Bar Car, just as before was over crowded, and Mr. Peters was in the middle of all of it, but saw Ryan walk in and waved to him.

Sidestepping and with lots of "Excuse me, excuse me please," Ryan was able to get next to the Conductor to ask him about the woman in car #1710, compartment B.

Checking in his book, the conductor said, "I'm sorry Mr. Ryan, but there are no women assigned to that compartment. There is Ralph Gore and Samuel Bamber and Mr. Bamber's son Jason."

"Mr. Peters. About Twenty minutes ago I tried to get the attention of a woman who was sitting in that compartment and she refused to let her face be seen, even after I tapped on the window."

"What would you like me to do, Mr. Ryan?"

"I would like for us to walk back to that car and check things out."

Pat stood there smiling and Ryan asked, "Care to join us Pat?"

"I'll be with you in a few seconds Robert I just need to check my messages on my phone."

The Conductor looked at both of them and said, "Let's head for the front of the train and I'll buy you both a coffee in the Conductor's Car."

"And where might that be Mr. Peters?" Ryan asked.

"The forward Baggage Car is split into two rooms. A sleeping compartment with a built-in kitchen and the other half is for storage. Hold on, I'll call Mr. Watts and ask him if he would put coffee on."

"How do you keep in contact with him, cell phone?"

The conductor pulled out a small compact sized gadget, held it up and said, "Mr. Watts, are you there?"

A few seconds passed and a response came back, "What can I do for you Mr. Peters?"

Ryan said, "Ask him if he would walk past compartment B in car #1710 and look at the passenger."

After hearing the request, Mr. Watts answered, "I just passed by that compartment and it's empty at the moment Mr. Peters."

Ryan shook his head and said, "I think we missed him."

7

Slowly walking forward to the Conductor's car, as Pat remained behind, they had walked through three cars looking at each passenger very closely, when Mr. Peters' phone started buzzing away.

Ryan asked, "Is that your cell or your communicator?"

"That is my cell phone Mr. Ryan. Excuse me, please, while I answer."

All Ryan could hear was, "Yes, yes, I understand, yes I'll get back to you. Yes, I'll call you back after I talk with Detective Ryan. No, he's a retired LA Detective. Give me five minutes and I'll call you back Sheriff."

Continuing to hold his cell phone in his hand, Mr. Peters told Ryan, "Well the imposter, the man who pretended to be me, was just pulled out of a shallow river called Johnson's Creek that runs under the railway trestle just outside of Grant New Mexico. We crossed over that trestle only about an hour and a half ago."

Looking confused, Ryan asked, "I know I'm going to hate myself for asking this, but how did that Sheriff know to call you, from just pulling a body out of the water?"

"You won't hate yourself, Detective and before you tell me again that you're retired, you are all we have in experience on this train and from what I've seen so far you still have some detective knowledge in your blood."

"It's ok Mr. Peters, I think you're correct in your assumption, now what did he say?"

"The man they pulled out of the water had on a conductor's uniform like mine with a name tag pinned on it that read, HEAD CONDUCTOR STANLEY PETERS."

Ryan crossed his arms in front of his chest and asked, "Anything else Mr. Peters?"

"The man was made up with facial make-up, artificial nose, eye brows, hair-piece, and padding, I assume to try and look like me."

Ryan seemed to gaze into space and said, "Come to think of it, when I first came in contact with him, he did resemble you a lot."

"It appears Detective, that we are dealing with people who were very prepared for what they intended to do."

"I think you're right Stanley, they are pros."

"Please Detective, let's keep it professional. I prefer Mr. Peters or Conductor Peters, if you please."

Ryan smiled and said, "As you wish, Mr. Peters. You want to call that Sheriff back and let me talk with him?"

Mr. Peters said, "As you wish, Detective."

"Mr. Peters, Let's make our way to that Conductor's Car before you call the Sheriff back."

Slowly walking and continuing to study each passenger's face, it didn't take long for Patricia Gibbs to catch up with the observant men as she joined them heading for the forward cars.

Apologizing for lagging behind so long, Pat said, "When nature calls, this lady always answers, gentlemen."

Arriving at the last passenger car going forward, before the Baggage/ Conductor's Car, the men looked for Mr. Watts who was nowhere to be found, so Mr. Peters called him on the train communicator, but there was no answer.

Leading the way by first opening the locked connecting car door, they stepped onto the platform between the two railway cars and closed the door behind them.

Mr. Peters then opened the door to the conductor's car with a special key on his key ring and then stepped aside to let Ryan and Patricia enter the car ahead of him.

At the far end of the car, in plain view they saw Mr. Watts seated at the table with his back to the wall.

Mr. Peters asked, "Mr. Watts, didn't you hear me calling you?" But there was no answer. His eyes just stared straight ahead.

Once again Mr. Peters asked, "Watts, what is the matter with you, can't you hear me?"

Walking over to the man, Ryan checked for a pulse on the man's neck and said, "He can't hear anybody anymore, he's dead."

With no visible signs of any violent force on Mr. Watts, it appeared that he just peacefully passed away at the table.

Stepping out from next to a wardrobe closet in the corner, Edward Taylor spoke softly and said, "Hello gentlemen, ma'am, would you kindly have a seat next to Mr. Watts?"

Looking much younger and healthier, Ed Taylor without any makeup or cosmetic accoutrements appeared to be closer to forty years old rather than seventy that he first professed to be and was holding a gun in his hand.

"What is the meaning of this?" Mr. Peters asked.

"Just shut up and sit down, you over-stuffed bellboy."

Ryan studied the man who had sat across from him in the compartment earlier and asked, "So what is it you want Taylor?"

"You also Detective, just sit down over there and shut up."

Sitting in silence, Ryan looked around at his surroundings. The walls and ceiling were painted in a pale yellow, with two large windows on each side of the car. Besides the table and chairs, a plush brown couch and matching recliner were against the opposite wall from the table. The floor in that section of the car had a dark gray indoor/outdoor low pile commercial carpet. A small oak cabinet, stove, and refrigerator were next to the table and chairs the threesome was seated in.

While sitting in the recliner, Ed Taylor's cell phone buzzed and he answered it immediately. From all appearances, it seemed that he was receiving instructions on what his next moves would be or someone reporting to him.

After ending the almost one sided conversation with the caller, Ed Taylor spoke to the conductor and asked him, "Are you familiar with the old water stop just west of Williams Junction, Mr. Peters?"

"Yes Sir I am."

"That's good, because that is where this train will make a short unscheduled stop and I will leave your company."

"That is impossible, Mr. Taylor."

"Mr. Peters, you will now arrange for the train to stop there, or you can join Mr. Watts in everlasting slumber. Do you understand what I'm telling you sir? Do it now."

Taking out his train communicator, Mr. Peters punched in two numbers and said, "Charlie we need to talk. Pick up Charlie."

In just a few seconds the response came back, "What's up Stanley, kind of busy up here."

Mr. Peters looked around and said, "We need to make a stop at Williams Junction Water Tower, Charlie."

"Why's that Stanley?"

"No questions Charlie. I will explain later."

"You need to explain now Stanley."

"Let me put it this way Charlie. If you don't stop where I told you to, someone will die. Now don't argue with me, just stop the train where I told you, over and out Charlie."

"Ok, *Mr. Peters*, you're in charge, but you get to answer to the higher-ups for this."

8

Twenty minutes had gone by with a calm and quiet mood that had been imposed by Ed Taylor; well, at least the quiet part of it was demanded by him. As for the calm, they tried to be as calm as they could be with a 9mm automatic pointed in their direction.

"Taylor, what are your intentions towards us?" Ryan asked.

"Detective, let me put your mind at ease. We have about two hours until we reach the water tower. Isn't that right Mr. Peters?"

"More like an hour and a half at our present speed Sir."

"Ok, an hour and a half give or take a few minutes. When the train stops, I will be getting off and you will be continuing on your way."

Ryan smiled slightly and asked, "Just like that. You jump off and we continue along like nothing ever happened?"

"Would you prefer some other way Detective?"

Ryan said, "Sounds good to me Taylor."

"Now Detective, if you would be so kind. You'll notice on the counter to your left, there are a dozen plastic tie straps. I would like you to get up slowly and use a couple of those straps to tie Mr. Peters' wrists to the arms of the captain's chair he is seated in."

The Conductor stood up and said, "I protest Sir. I will not be treated in this fashion."

"Sit down Mr. Peters, or I will make it un-necessary for you to be tied at all. Please, down sir."

Reluctantly obeying the command, the now red-faced conductor sat back down and watched as his wrists were strapped to the chair arms.

Looking at the woman, Ed Taylor asked, "And what is your name dear?"

She responded, "Patricia Gibbs, you asshole."

"Well Miss Gibbs, I hope you paid attention to the detective in the way he used those plastic tie straps?"

"I did."

"Good. Now Detective, I want you to switch chairs with Miss Gibbs, since her chair has arms like Mr. Peters' chair. Then Miss, I would like you to strap the detective's wrists to the arms of his chair. Do it now Miss Gibbs."

After she completed her task, Patricia was instructed to make some coffee and Ed Taylor finished the job of tying the two men to their chairs by strapping their ankles to the legs of the chairs.

Feeling obviously more relaxed, Taylor sat back down in the recliner and asked, "How do you like your coffee, gentlemen? Just ask the lady and I'm sure she with get it for you."

Over the next half hour, Ryan tried to get any information possible from his captor, but it was to no avail, with any questions asked, they were only answered with questions and laughter.

With both of the Conductor's communication devices lying on the table, it was easy for all to see when the cell phone started vibrating and the ID read, "Gallup PD."

As Ed Taylor got up from the recliner, he first studied the read-out on the phone and then calmly asked Miss Gibbs, "Would you please join me here at the table dear?"

Holding his weapon firmly against Patricia's head he instructed, "First, Miss Gibbs, you will hold the phone for Mr. Peters. Sir, you will answer and not say anything that would make this nice young lady get her brains splattered all over this car. Is that under stood, Mr. Peters?"

Answering the phone the Conductor said, "Peters here, can I help you?"

"Yes, this is Lieutenant Howard Steel, of the Gallup Police Department. Is this the Conductor in charge of the train?"

"Yes it is Lieutenant, what can I do for you?"

"The Chief wanted me to call you and let you know that everything will be in place at the time of your arrival. Have there been any further developments?"

"No there hasn't been anything new to report. If you please Lieutenant, I have passengers to attend to. I will see you when we arrive in Gallup, thank you and good bye."

After hitting the END button, Pat placed the cell phone back on the table and sat down.

Releasing the firm hold he had on Patricia's hair, Ed Taylor sat back down in the recliner and said, "See how smoothly things can go when we all cooperate and work together."

Ryan just couldn't resist so he had to ask, "So Taylor, the guy you threw off the train into the river refused to cooperate with you?"

"Let's get a couple things straight Det. Ryan. The more you know, the less chance you have of surviving this trip. I will give you this so you know

40

who it is that spared your life and the life of that oversized bellhop you're sitting next to. My name is Richard Price and this is not the last time we will be face to face. At some time Det. Ryan I will take your useless life away from you. You won't see it coming and you won't be able to avoid it, but just know that I'll be out there. As far as the fat conductor impersonator goes, let's just say the gentleman chose his own agenda and failed in his assigned mission, so let's just leave it at that."

9

Approximately fifteen minutes away from the water tower, Richard Price got up from the recliner where he had been resting and preparing his next moves.

Walking over to the table he picked up the train communicator, looked at the conductor and said, "Mr. Peters, you will instruct the engineer to stop the train at the water tower with the engine directly next to the tower. He will remain there exactly two minutes and then continue on his way to Gallup."

"And why will I do all this that you ask sir?"

Let me put it this way Mr. Peters. You will do what I say or I will first cut her throat, put a bullet in the detective's head and then enjoy cutting your heart out, understood?"

Ryan spoke up and said, "If it were my choice, plan one sounds more to my liking. Don't you agree Pat?"

"Just do what the man asks Mr. Peters and stop screwing around trying to get us all killed." Miss Gibbs said.

"Very well, bring the communicator over here and push the three and then the zero and hold it up so I can speak into the damn thing."

"Charlie, pick up Charlie. I have additional information on our unscheduled stop."

A few more seconds went by when Charlie answered. "Okay Stanley, whatcha got?"

"When you stop at the water tower, you will align the engine exactly with the tower and remain there two minutes. You will then start the train moving and continue on to Gallup. Charlie, if you do it exactly as I say, there will be no loss of life. Do not contact the authorities. You got it Charlie?"

"You better know what you're doing Stan, because there will be a lot of shit to pay."

A few more minutes passed by and the train began its slow decrease in speed and Richard Price prepared for his exit. Holding Mr. Peters' ring of keys in his left hand and once again the 9mm in his right, he instructed Miss. Gibbs, "You will be coming with me my dear, just in case someone planned a trap for me."

While Ryan and the conductor both protested, Taylor said, "I will release this woman after I am safely away from the train, gentlemen, so shut up and sit there waiting for someone to rescue you in Gallup." Looking at Ryan, Price said, "I look forward to our next meeting, Det. Ryan."

As the train came to a complete stop, Price and Miss Gibbs stepped off the train and walked to a waiting car.

Getting into the rear seat of the black Cadillac limo with the blacked out windows, Price looked at Patricia Gibbs and said, "That went well Beverly; they never suspected you were part of the operation."

The woman previously known as Patricia Gibbs said, "And you Richard, it was hard remembering not to call you by your real name at first."

Watching the train pull away, Richard Price then instructed the driver, "Head for Los Angeles, Jim."

10

The train traveled slowly down the track, never getting up to full speed. The engineer, trying several times for a response on the communicator, finally made a decision to stop the train and investigate on his own.

With much caution, Charlie Briscoe climbed the steps of the Conductors car and looked through the door window.

Seeing both Mr. Peters and Bob Ryan secured to their chairs, he slowly opened the door and before he could say a word, he heard, "It's ok Charlie, he's gone, come and cut these ties on us please."

"What the hell went on here?"

"Long story Charlie, but first look in the top drawer in the sink cabinet you'll find a pair of snips. Please be careful while you cut us free."

Upon being separated from the chair, Mr. Peters grabbed his cell phone from the table and redialed the last call number that came in, Lt. Howard Steel, Gallup Police Dept.

With a description given by the conductor, the lieutenant put out the order to apprehend with caution Richard Price, for questioning.

Approximately fifteen minutes later the West Coast Flyer pulled in to the Gallup Train Station and was met by more police officers and newsmen then were needed.

The train was held at the station for six hours while the Gallup Forensic Team examined the train compartment, but only after the County Coroner completed his examination on the body of John Stafford.

The Conductors car was also examined for fingerprints and any other clues that could lead to the apprehension of Richard Price.

Bob Ryan and Mr. Peters were also questioned extensively for any additional information.

As the train pulled out of the Gallup Train Station, Ryan sat quietly sipping his coffee in the rear bar car, now that half the passengers had decided to continue their journey in the secure comfort of their compartments.

It was 4 am and it was a cool dark morning outside but in the warmth of the bar car Ryan thought if he could just catch a couple of hours sleep, the mild fog in his head would dissipate and life would go on as usual.

Deciding to return to his compartment to try to catch those few winks of sleep before the train arrived at its next stop in Flagstaff, Arizona, he got up from his seat and walked slowly, not willingly but showing how his years and fatigue had caught up with him.

The car before his own, Ryan came across Mr. Peters, who was comforting an older woman and her grandchild, letting them know that everything was fine and that we would be in Flagstaff by 7am.

With just a wink and a smile, Ryan then said, "Goodnight Stanley."

Returning the gesture, Mr. Peters said, "Rest comfortably Robert, I'll come by your compartment when we arrive in Flagstaff with some fresh coffee."

"Thank you Sir,"

Reaching his now empty compartment he realized that all his belongings were still in the Conductors car where he had brought them earlier, but as he opened the small closet to hang his jacket he saw his carry-on bag and he smiled and thought, "Thank you Stanley." Now riding alone in his own compartment since Chris Heschel's departure in

Gallup, Ryan kicked off his shoes, piled up a bunch of pillows and retrieved his book from his carry-on bag.

Looking for his slip of paper that marked the chapter where he had left off reading The DiVinci Codes, he found two papers folded and placed in the center of his book.

The first page was a hand written note instructing Ryan to please make sure the following page was given to the proper authorities. It contained evidence that one of the largest pharmaceutical manufacturers in the world is planning to market a cholesterol medication that would have long term health effects on its users.

The copy of the report showed in detail how one of the ingredients was derived from plants only grown in Africa, but was now being cultivated in the swamps of Louisiana.

The plant ingredient being used would eventually eat away a person's intestines and the FDA was being mislead.

Reading the report, Ryan realized that John Stafford's death involved much more then anyone would ever know, unless he exposed what he had just found out. Knowing that the smart and proper thing to do was to turn over the two pieces of paper to the proper authorities, Ryan decided first it was time to catch up on those few winks of sleep he desperately needed.

11

The knocking on the compartment door startled Ryan awake and he couldn't imagine who would be trying to get his attention since he felt like he had fallen asleep only seconds earlier.

Opening his eyes the overly tired ex detective realized that it was already morning and after looking at his wristwatch he saw that six hours had gone by since putting his head down on the pillow.

Mr. Peters greeted Ryan as he opened the door and offered him the tray he was carrying that contained pastries, croissants, orange juice and coffee.

Ryan asked, "Care to join me Mr. Peters?"

"Mr. Ryan, I have so many things to attend to, but I will see you when we arrive in Flagstaff, which should be in about one hour. Enjoy your breakfast."

"Thank you I hope we can talk later?"

"I will be getting additional help to replace Mr. Watts when we arrive in Flagstaff, then I should have some free time for us to talk."

After placing the tray on the foldout table, Ryan grabbed a few things from his carry-on bag and made his way to the restroom.

Looking into the mirror above the sink, the image Ryan saw looking back at him was that of an old man, a tired unshaven weather-worn man who had been through a lot in the past two days.

At sixty-four years old, the once strong out spoken enforcer of the law was in the possession of information that he knew was dangerous to whoever tried to interfere with the plans of its designers.

Shaving off the burly gray whisker stubs on his face, splashing on some cold water and combing back his thinning hair, he looked into his own eyes and said, "I'm getting too old for this shit."

Returning to his compartment Ryan put on a clean shirt and stuffed all his belongings into his carry-on bag.

While the train was stopped in Flagstaff, Ryan made the decision that he needed to turn over the papers he had in his possession to the FBI and let them figure out what to do with them.

After a quick handshake and well wishes to Stanley Peters, Ryan made a phone call to the local FBI and arranged a meeting with one of their agents.

The meeting would take place at the Flagstaff Airport and then Ryan would get on a flight to Los Angeles and put everything behind him, or so he thought.

Agent Roland Holloway met with Ryan at the Southwest terminal of the airport and after filling the agent in on the past couple of days of problems, Ryan handed Agent Holloway an envelope containing the report entrusted to him.

The one thing Ryan didn't tell the agent was that he had made copies of the report using a copy machine at one of the ticket counters after showing his badge and ID. He then folded and filed them back in his copy of The Da Vinci Codes for safe keeping.

Something Ryan learned through all his years of police work was that when you are not sure of what you were doing, back yourself up, either with sufficient help from people you trusted or documentation to protect your own ass.

12

The flight from Flagstaff to Los Angeles took less than two hours. Unfortunately the trip through the airport and the car rental agency, plus the backed up traffic on the freeway to the San Fernando Valley took much longer.

Arrangements had already been made for a place for Ryan to stay until he found a home of his own. Knowing the Valley like the back of his hand, Ryan had no problem finding his destination.

Dorothy Metzger was an old friend and widow of Ryan's ex-partner Leo when they were with the LAPD years earlier.

When Robert (as she called him) called and told her he was moving back to LA, she insisted that he stay with her during his home search for as much time as he needed.

Dorothy's home was located in the western section of the valley in Woodland Hills, just far enough from downtown Los Angeles to make a person feel like they were far from the crime of the city. Not that the Valley didn't have its own crime problems, but just not as horrific.

After a warm welcome, the two old friends went to the kitchen and Dorothy poured them both a cup of coffee and then she suggested they sit on the porch and catch up a little.

Sitting on the front porch in the shade of a large walnut tree, with Dorothy, and enjoying a cup of coffee as they reminisced about the past, gave Ryan a good feeling of being home.

When he packed up and moved to Florida only four years earlier, Ryan had sold his house for what he thought was an obscene amount of money, but in today's housing market it couldn't buy him a small shack.

While living in Florida Ryan rented a small condominium near the beach and the money he received for the sale of his California home was placed in a T-BILL account where it could gain interest and be there for the future.

Dorothy told Ryan she was considering selling her house and finding something a little smaller and easier to maintain because the cost for taxes, utilities and just normal maintenance was eating away at her savings and Leo's pension.

Ryan asked her to consider renting him the guesthouse above the garage, which would provide her with a little extra income if the place was available.

Dorothy agreed but only if Ryan would treat the rest of the property like his own and she do all the cooking for both of them.

Ryan thought for a few seconds and said, "You drive a hard bargain Dot, but I know you're a damn good cook and I would have to be crazy to refuse your hospitality."

Dorothy said, "Good. Tonight you can sleep in the spare room upstairs, and tomorrow you can start getting the guesthouse ready for yourself. And Robert, it's going to need some serious cleaning, because it hasn't been used in many years."

"I'm sure it will be fine Dot, and thank you dear."

"Welcome home Robert."

"I think I'll go and check it out before it gets too dark out."

While climbing up the steps leading to the large two-bedroom guesthouse, Ryan's cell phone started buzzing and the caller ID read, UNKNOWN.

The caller identified himself as Agent John Simmons of the Flagstaff FBI office and he informed Ryan that Agent Holloway had not been heard from since his meeting with Ryan at the airport in Flagstaff.

Explaining to the agent what his meeting with Holloway was about, Ryan then told Agent Simmons, "That was the last time I saw him or had any contact with him."

The agent also asked if Ryan had any communication with Stanley Peters, a Conductor for the railroad.

Telling the agent that the last time he spoke with Mr. Peters was around 7 am that morning brought a response of, "I'm sorry to say that Mr. Peters was found this morning on the train in the Conductor's quarters with his throat cut and appeared to be dead for a couple of hours."

Deciding it was time for him to verify the identity of the caller, Ryan asked him for the office number and told him he would call him right back. After hanging up Ryan called information and got the phone number for the Flagstaff FBI office and returned the call, asking for Agent Simmons.

After talking with the operator at the FBI Ryan was turned over to an Agent William Lacey, who informed Ryan, "I'm sorry Sir, but we do not have an Agent Simmons in our office. What is it that I can help you with?"

"Do you have an Agent Holloway at your office?"

"Yes we do, but he is out of the office right now. I'll ask you once again Sir. What does this concern?"

"Agent Lacey is it?'

"Yes Sir."

"It is very important that you try and locate Agent Holloway. I have a suspicion that he is in grave danger."

"Sir, this is a very busy office, and I think--"
"Look you idiot, Holloway may be dead already. Now if this is too much for you to handle, you better put one of your Supervisors on before I give you more shit than you want to hear."

"Hold on there wise guy and I'll get you someone else."

13

As Ryan sat at the top of the steps to the guesthouse holding his cell phone, he felt after fifteen minutes of waiting on hold that he was being completely ignored.

With his temper flaring and the little hairs on the back of his neck rising, Ryan made one more call.

Pressing re-dial, once again he got through to the operator at the Flagstaff FBI office.

Ryan said, "My name is Robert Ryan. Please turn on your recorder. I believe Agent Roland Holloway has been murdered. My cell phone number is 818-555-6969. If someone is interested, call me."

"Sir, you need to talk with an Agent."

"Lady, I already talked with an Agent. Now please pass that message on to one of the Supervisors."

After pressing the END button on his cell, Ryan mumbled the words, "Damn fools."

Clipping his phone back on his belt Ryan got up and walked through the door of his new home in California.

With its two large skylights and the fluorescent lights that went on when he flicked the switch, every cobweb in the front room lit up brightly.

The floor in the front room was covered from wall to wall with black and red linoleum squares and the walls were painted a light gray with white trim.

In the far left corner there sat a hexagon card table with a fitted brown cover that protected it from the thick dust that had accumulated over the years.

A TV on a rotating stand sat in the far right corner with a tan sectional couch positioned directly in front of it.

Unfortunately the couch was not covered and would require a heavy-duty vacuum cleaner and extra bags for the mounds of dust.

Looking to his left covered partially with a tarp, Ryan spotted something he remembered from visits many years ago when he and several other officers played poker there in the newly furnished guesthouse that Leo was so proud of.

A built-in bar with running water and a refrigerator was something his ex-partner was also very proud of, even though he drank alcoholic beverages so seldom. He enjoyed providing the drinks for his guests.

The right front corner of the room was Leo's spot for when he would drop out of the poker games.

Two book cases fit in the corner at each side of a big cushioned high back chair and a hanging lamp that gave just the right amount of light for reading. Leo called it his comfort corner and everyone knew it was a hands-off, butt-off seat for him alone.

As Ryan walked across the room he saw that no one had been up there in quite some time by the footprints he was leaving behind him on the dusty floor. The door next to the card table led to a storage room that contained a few boxes, several file cabinets, a couple extra chairs, several pictures in very old frames and a shit load of dust.

The second door next to the TV led to the bedroom that was small with a full sized bed, a dresser, one nightstand and a built-in closet in the far corner. The carpeting on the floor appeared to be a very dark blue but with all the dust it was hard to tell.

The walls and ceiling were painted an off white and the two windows had white blinds and light blue drapes that matched the bed spread.

Next to the built-in closet a door led to the very small bathroom with a stall shower, pedestal sink and a commode that needed replacing because of a cracked tank.

The walls also would need repainting because there was no way Ryan was going to sit and crap every morning looking at pink wallpaper with little white ducks on it. The wallpaper with the little ducks was a small touch Dorothy added one weekend when Leo was out of town as a joke.

Standing in the bedroom doorway admiring his new home he felt his phone vibrate before the first buzz.

The caller ID read, "FBI."

Answering he said, "Ryan here, can I help you?"

"Mr. Ryan, this is Senior Agent Tad Billings."

"Yes Sir, what can I do for you Sir?"

"Well Mr. Ryan, you can start by explaining your earlier phone call."

"Well Agent Billings, it all started when I called your office early this morning and explained to Agent Holloway about a report I had in my possession and wanted to turn over to your office."

"Let's cut to the chase Mr. Ryan. I know you met with Agent Holloway at the Flagstaff Airport, and I assume you turned over the documents you had to him. Unfortunately we have no way of confirming that because the Agent has disappeared and we have not had any contact with him whatsoever."

"Sir, when I tried earlier to inform your office of what had happened I had to deal with an idiot agent named Lacey who passed me off to dead air and I sat for ten minutes before I called again and left my message. That is why sir I made the second call and pushed the envelope the way I did. It was to get someone with a higher IQ to pay attention."

"Mr. Ryan you have my attention and I promise you that you will not be ignored again and I apologize for Agent Lacey's inappropriate behavior."

14

As Ryan started to explain the circumstances of the day, the agent stopped him politely saying,

"With all due respect to the service you had provided while you were a member of the LAPD, I have to inform you that you are wanted for questioning in the death of Stanley Peters.

"WHAT?"

"Mr. Ryan, from what the investigating agent found out by questioning other passengers on the train, you happened to be the last person to see Mr. Peters alive."

"Sir, with all due respect to you and your team of agents, you guys are out of your fucking minds."

"Maybe so Mr. Ryan, but we need you to report to the LA office of the FBI and turn yourself in for questioning."

Agreeing to report to the FBI office in the morning was not something that Ryan wanted to do but he knew that if he didn't, they would come and find him. Reluctantly Ryan said, "Agent Billings, I'll be there at ten if that's all right with you?"

"That will work just fine Mr. Ryan just give your name at the front desk in the lobby."

Because of Ryan's long absence, Dorothy decided to come out to the guesthouse and look for him. Finding her new boarder sitting at the top of the steps just staring into space, she climbed the steps and asked, "Something personal Robert, or is it something you want to share?"

"You know Dot, the profession Leo and I chose is one that stays with you for the rest of your life. There is no such thing as retiring from law enforcement; it gets in your blood and it stays there until you die. I'm sorry Dot, I didn't mean to say that in that way."

"It's ok Robert, I understand. Leo always said that once a cop always a cop. Just do it the best you can."

"I really miss his patience and wisdom at times like this."

Putting her hand on his shoulder Dorothy said, "Me too Robert, me too. Is it something I can help with?"

I think the only one who can help me is a good lawyer Dot. You happen to know one?"

"Sorry Robert, but that's something I don't know."

15

Sleeping in a freshly made bed in the main house was something Ryan was not accustomed to. The sheets not only felt soft as a baby's bottom, but also smelled like a fresh spring morning in the country.

The other fragrances he noticed upon awakening that permeated the air were those of bacon cooking and just a hint of freshly brewed coffee. Ryan knew that Dorothy was doing what she liked to do best in the kitchen, fine cooking with lots of heart.

Ryan decided to just lie in the bed for a little while longer. As he tuned in the clock radio to a local mild jazz station, he noticed the time was only 7 am, so he gave himself another twenty minutes before he got up.

Finding the robe that Dorothy had placed at the foot of the bed for him to use, Ryan slipped it on and walked down stairs to get a better look at what his new landlord had cooking that was sending out all the wonderful smells.

With a big smile on her face Dot greeted him with, "Well good morning Robert. Slept well I hope?"

"The best night's sleep I've had in a long time, Dot."

"I hope you brought a big appetite down with you and don't you dare tell me, just coffee please."

"Is that pancakes I see there Dot?"

"Pancakes, eggs, bacon, hash browns. If you don't see something you like, just ask. Robert, I have a full refrigerator and the desire to cook to your heart's content."

"How about I start out with coffee and then a little sample of everything you cooked up, Dot?"

"Now that's what I wanted to hear. How about a glass of orange juice to top it off?"

"Sounds fine Dot."

As Ryan slowly worked away at more breakfast than he had eaten in years, Dorothy asked, "So Robert what are your plans for your first day back in California?"

"Well after I put myself together I have to pay a visit to the FBI office down on Wilshire Blvd."

Before Dorothy had a chance to respond, the chimes of the front door bell alerted them to a visitor.

Walking to the front door, Dorothy could see two people through the window in the door, but couldn't identity either of them through the thin white curtains.

Slightly moving one of the curtains aside she could see one of the visitors holding his ID up to the glass.

Opening the door she asked, "Can I help you?"

"Yes ma'am, I'm Agent Cisco and this is my partner Agent Reynolds. By any chance is Robert Ryan here?"

"May I ask what this is about?"

"You may ma'am but this concerns Mr. Ryan and a confidential matter. Is he here ma'am?"

Turning and pointing to the couch, Dorothy said, "Have a seat and I'll see if he's available."

The lead Agent responded with, "We'll be fine right here ma'am, thank you."

Walking back into the kitchen, Dorothy said, "You have visitors Robert."

"Who is it, Dot?"

"A good looking man and a pretty woman, and they're both wearing suits. They're FBI Robert. They showed me their ID's through the window."

"They couldn't wait for me to come to them, damn pushy bastards."

"Now Robert, hold your temper."

"Would you do me a favor Dot?"

"What do you need dear?"

"Tell the happy two-some out there that I'm going up to my room to get dressed and I'll be with them in about fifteen minutes. I'll go up the back stairs. Bring them a couple of bottles of water please."

Surprised Dorothy asked, "Water?"

"Yeah, it's a long ride to the Wilshire office with lots of traffic I hope."

"Oh you're bad, Robert."

"Got any salty pretzels?"

"Go get dressed, will you. I'll get the water and the pretzels."

Walking back to the living room Dorothy found the agents standing right where they were when she went to the kitchen.

Setting a large bowl of pretzels on the coffee table, she then looked at the two staring at her and she said, "You can stand there if you want, but Robert won't be done dressing for about fifteen or twenty minutes."

"Mr. Ryan does know that we are here?"

"Yes he does. He will be down in fifteen or twenty minutes like I said. Have a seat please you're letting the flies in."

The woman agent said, "Thank you ma'am."

"I'll be right back, help your self to the pretzels."

Going into the kitchen, Dorothy soon returned carrying three bottles of water and placed them on the glass coffee table in front of the agents.

Taking one of the bottles and opening it, Dorothy sat down in the recliner chair across from the agents who were now sitting on the couch and asked, "So what's going on?"

"Like I said before ma'am, it's a matter between Mr. Ryan and the Bureau."

"You know Agent Cisco, my husband, may he rest in peace, was with the LAPD for many years before he was killed by some madman who was systematically killing people."

"Yes ma'am, I am aware of that, and I'm sorry for your loss. From what I've heard he was a good man and a fine officer."

"Thank you Agent Cisco, please have something to drink, it's awfully dry here in the Valley."

As agent Reynolds reached for a bottle of water she said, "Thank you ma'am, you have a beautiful home."

"Why thank you Agent Reynolds, it's been in my husband's family for many years and I have grown to love it."

The agent asked, "How many rooms are there?"

"Actually more rooms than I need dear. I was considering selling but Robert talked me out of it. He will be renting the apartment above the garage and the income will help me to pay the expenses for the up-keep."

Agent Reynolds asked, "How long have you lived here?"

"About twenty-five years dear."

As the conversation went on about the house and the neighborhood the time passed by quickly and before they knew it Ryan was walking down the winding staircase into the large front hall.

The agents had finished their water, snacked on a few pretzels and were ready for a talk with the man they came to see.

Walking into the living room Ryan asked, "I guess you're my ride down to Wilshire Blvd?"

16

As they drove east on the Ventura Freeway for approximately seven miles before merging onto the 405 south, not a word was spoken. Finally Ryan broke the ice and asked, "So, both of you born and raised in California?"

With no response other then a stare from the female agent in the passenger seat, he decided to try again.

"You know, it always helps in situations like this to be a little sociable, don't you think?"

Again there was no response from either agent. Trying another approach Ryan said, "I will be sure to tell your supervisor how I tried to open up to you two assholes but unfortunately that stiff stick up your asses wouldn't let you bend a little."

Turning to face him, the female agent finally broke her silence and said, "We've been warned about you Ryan. Anyone who talks to you either dies or disappears!"

Smiling a little, Ryan said, "Nothing like a woman with a big mouth and a badge who is also an asshole."

That did it! Agent Reynolds lost her cool for a few seconds and asked Ryan why he couldn't keep his old aging ass in Florida and stay retired and maybe, just maybe, there would be fewer dead people and missing agents.

Ryan leaned forward in the seat and said, "Look you dumb shit. I was minding my own business when all of this was dropped on me. I turned over what I had to one of your cohorts and he disappeared. The people I was on the train with seem to be dying off because your people can't find out what the hell is going on. And you want to blame me. Well fuck off Agent Reynolds, it's in your lap now, I'm just a civilian caught up in all this shit."

With no response, the silence started once again as the traffic backed up on the 405 Freeway and the Wilshire Blvd. exit was still a long ways off.

So sitting back and taking in some of the beautiful scenery nature had provided, that is with a little help from Cal Trans and the tree trimmers, Ryan just watched as they finally made it up to Mulholand Drive. Now that might seem like they traveled a long distance, but in reality they only covered about one mile since merging from the Ventura Freeway.

It is very common for the 405 freeway to back up at any given time of day, but on this day it was almost a sure thing that there had been an accident somewhere up ahead.

Another half hour passed by and the vehicle that was moving at a snail's pace had only made it as far as The Getty Center Drive, which meant, half mile, half hour.

With all the vehicles on the road now completely at a stop, the driver, Agent Cisco put the car in park and looked over his right shoulder and asked, "Looks like we are going to be spending a lot more time with you than expected Ryan, so why not tell us what really happened?"

"Is it something you really want to hear, or am I just wasting my time?"

Before Agent Cisco could respond, his partner opened up once again, "Only if it's the truth Ryan."

Ryan's sharp tongue blasted again, "You know Reynolds, sometimes you have to listen with your ears instead of your ass and then the truth is easier to hear."

Agent Cisco's stare was enough to get his partner to close her mouth and let Ryan continue.

Very calmly Ryan asked, "What do you have, an on and off switch on her?"

Agent Cisco said, "Don't push your luck Ryan, either tell us your version or sit back and enjoy the rest of the trip."

"Right to the point Cisco, that's what I like. Okay, I'm assuming you heard about all that went down on the train?"

"Yeah, we read the report."

"I met with an Agent Holloway at Flagstaff Airport and turned over some papers that were passed on to me by one of the dead guys on the train. It seems that these papers show that one of the big pharmaceutical companies is ready to put a pill on the market that will reduce cholesterol better than any other product available today. Problem is, the shit will eventually kill you by eating away at your intestines."

"And you had proof of this?"

"Hey, I didn't know what the hell it was all about. So I turned it over to one of your guys and he disappeared."

"What about those people on the train, who killed them?"

"Looks like a nutcase named Price, Richard Price, if that's his real name. He's one dangerous character. Uses disguises in a very professional way. Shit, that could be him sitting next to you.

Agent Reynolds turned her head slightly and gave Ryan a one-finger salute and said, "Rotate."

"You express yourself so eloquently, Agent Reynolds."

As the traffic started to move again, Agent Cisco said, "Maybe we should continue this later after you talk with Supervisor John Crane?"

"That's who you're taking me to see?"

"Yes. He's a good man and a decent senior agent. Just be straight with him and we'll be driving you back home."

The traffic speed started to pick up and in a matter of minutes they were exiting at Wilshire Blvd. and a few more minutes and they were pulling into the parking lot of the Federal Building.

As Agent Reynolds opened the door for Ryan to get out of the vehicle, the ex detective held out his hand and said, "Truce, Agent Reynolds?"

Reynolds looked at him and said, "Why not? Truce, Ryan," and then they shook hands.

17

While riding up in the elevator to the FBI offices, Agent Reynolds asked, "So Ryan, how long did you serve the city on the LAPD?"

"Seems like most of my life Reynolds, but on and off it was around twenty-eight years."

"You took an early retirement, at what, sixty-two?"

"Actually I was fifty-eight."

"So you took the oath at a late age."

"After four years of college, I decided with the help of Uncle Sam, that I needed to see more of the world. So after training in South Carolina it was determined that a visit to Vietnam was in order."

As the elevator opened Ryan said, "Maybe we can finish our walk down memory lane a little later."

With a smile on her face, Agent Reynolds said, "Sounds good, Ryan."

Stepping out of the elevator, the first thing that struck Ryan's eyesight was a large shield on the wall informing all who entered that floor that they were on Federal property, and it was the Federal Bureau of Investigation.

The receptionist, a young woman around twenty-five, smiled and said, "The Bureau Chief is expecting you. I'll let him know you're here."

After a short conversation with the Chief, the receptionist told the trio, "Please have a seat in Conference Room One and Bureau Chief John Crane will join you in a few minutes."

Before the agents or Ryan had a chance to sit at the long conference table, they were joined by Chief Crane, a tall striking man around fifty, dressed in a light gray suit, slightly graying hair and looking so much like Clint Eastwood, that he could be his younger brother.

Holding out his hand to Ryan he said, "Thank you for joining us this morning Mr. Ryan, I hope it wasn't, too much of an inconvenience for you, please sit."

Ryan said, "Thank you Chief, I would like to help you in any way I can."

"What can I do to make you more comfortable Mr. Ryan? We have coffee, Danishes, water, you name it."

At first Ryan thought of saying no, but then said, "What the hell, I would like a cup of coffee and piece of Danish if that wouldn't be too much trouble since my nice country breakfast was interrupted earlier?"

The Chief looked at Agent Cisco and asked, "Agent Cisco, would you see what you can scout up for Mr. Ryan, and I would like a cup of coffee also if you please."

Ryan sat back in his chair and said, "Thank you Sir."

"Mr. Ryan, I hope Agents Cisco and Reynolds filled you in on why your presence was requested here this morning?"

Looking across the table at Agent Reynolds, the corners of Ryan's mouth turned up slightly and answered, "Yes Sir, particularly Agent Reynolds. She was very exact and to the point about why you needed to speak with me, and apologized for the early-unexpected conference this morning. My intentions were to get myself settled in at my new living quarters and then pay you a visit this morning, but this is fine. So what do you need from me Chief?"

"Well Mr. Ryan, in order to put things in perspective, I am going to need a complete account of everything and everyone you came in contact with from the time you boarded the train in New Mexico. Our conversation will be recorded, and at any time, if you feel that you need legal representation, we will stop until it is provided for you. In other words, Mr. Ryan, and please don't take this in the wrong way, you have the right to remain silent. If you give up that right, anything you say can be used against you in a court of law. You have the right to an attorney; if you cannot afford an attorney one will be appointed to you. Do you understand these rights?"

"You know Sir. I have spoken those words so many times over my almost thirty years with the LAPD and in most cases it was to some asshole who was as guilty as shit. I understand what you're saying Chief, so let me have my coffee and cake, and let's get on with the statement."

"Thank you Mr. Ryan, let's do it."

18

After four grueling hours of questions and explanations, Ryan and Agent Reynolds were standing in front of the elevator waiting to return to the world below.

Bureau Chief John Crane appeared very satisfied with the ex-detective's co-operation and informed him that he may be needed for additional information at a later date.

Ryan's memory not being as sharp as it was in his younger days made it hard to recall every moment of his train ride from New Mexico. Drawing on his experience, however, as a detective for those many years helped him through recalling important facts about the trip.

Even now, as he was about to board the elevator he recalled that Richard Price had a large discolored scar on the top of his right hand and informed Agent Reynolds.

Driving back to the West Valley, Agent Reynolds and Ryan had west a more upbeat conversation than the earlier attack on each other's character, but still a little cold.

Ryan asked her, "So Reynolds, do you have a first name or do your friends call you Agent also?"

"My first name is of no concern to you, Mr. Ryan."

"Fine, I'll just keep calling you Reynolds. So Reynolds, were you born and raised in California?"

"Sir, I don't believe that information will help our investigation in any way."

"Been with the Bureau a long time Reynolds?"

"Again Sir that is not something I wish to discuss with you."

"You're a real tight ass, huh Reynolds? I know, I know. Not something you want to divulge at this time, maybe when we become a little closer?"

Pulling into the circular driveway at Dorothy Metzger's home, the car came to a stop in front of the steps leading to the front door. Before getting out of the car, Ryan turned to his driver and said,

"I want to thank you for a most memorable drive Agent Reynolds, and please visit again."

"It's Barbara."

"Thank you Barbara, nice to meet you."

Standing on the front porch ringing the door bell, Ryan grew tired of waiting for Dorothy to answer so he walked around to the back and headed for the stairs leading to the guest house.

Looking at the back door to the house, he noticed that the window next to the door handle was broken and the door was partially open.

Slowly walking up the back porch steps, Ryan put a little pressure on the door and it opened with a creaking noise.

The porch ran the entire width of the back of the house and had a couple of tables on each side of a back door leading into the kitchen.

Though the Sun had not gone down yet the porch was very dark because of a large over grown tree that shaded most of the rear of the house plus dirty screens that were in need of repair.

When Ryan tried to open the door he found it too had been broken into, noticing the splintered wood lying on the floor around the threshold.

Pushing open the door he called out, "Dot, are you home? Dot, it's Robert. But there was no answer.

Dorothy Metzger's kitchen was an old fashioned cook's kitchen, its paint a faded yellow with white counter tops and a large six-burner cook's stove with a double side-by-side oven.

A very large four-door refrigerator was built into the left wall and a walk in pantry was located just a couple of steps to its right. On the right wall below an extra wide garden window a large stainless steel triple sink was set into the counter.

To the right of the sink in a large wooden block Ryan saw just what he was looking for, an entire collection of Chicago Cutlery with knives ranging from the smallest paring knife to an over- sized meat cleaver.

Grabbing the meat cleaver and walking into the dinning room, Ryan once again shouted out, "Dot, its Robert." And again there was no answer.

Deciding to pass up the rear stairs from the kitchen to the second floor, Ryan slowly started up the main staircase in the front hall.

Halfway up the stairs the front door opened and Dorothy Metzger looked up at Ryan and asked, "Robert, what the hell are you doing with that cleaver in your hand?"

"Stay where you are Dot, there may be an intruder in the house."

Startled by what he had said, Dorothy asked, "Why do you think that Robert?"

"The back porch door and the kitchen door have both been broken in."

"Have you called the police yet?"

"I just got home about five minutes ago."

"Is that a yes?"

"No, it's a no, you better call 911. I'm going to look upstairs."

Continuing up the stairs Ryan looked first to see if any of the bedroom doors were open, and to his surprise every door, including the one leading up to the attic was wide open.

Walking slowly past each doorway he looked inside and saw nothing unusual until he got to the guest room he was using. The carry-on bag had been dumped on the bed and all his belongings were scattered on the floor. The copy of The Da Vinci Code was lying open on the bed and the copies of the report were gone.

By the time Ryan came back down the rear staircase into the kitchen, a police car had arrived and one of the officers was talking with Dorothy in the driveway.

As Ryan walked from the kitchen through the dining room, he surprised the young officer who instantly removed his weapon from its holster and said, "Hold it there."

"Ryan responded, "Easy Junior, I live here."

Before lowering his weapon the officer asked, "And what is your name Sir, and may I see some ID please?"

Ryan said, "Robert Ryan, son, as he slowly reached behind to remove his wallet to show the officer his ID.

The officer said, "Do that slowly sir."

Ryan said, "Its okay son. I'm just getting my ID."

"Well Mr. Ryan, first of all I'm not your son and second my name is Officer Peter Kurtz, not junior. Now what is your involvement in all of this?"

Ryan smiled and said, "Just a boarder, officer just a boarder."

Looking at Dorothy who had walked up behind the officer, Ryan said, "Dot, I have to call those people who picked me up this morning. Hopefully Officer Kurtz will call in and get a detective out here to check things out."

As the officer started to say something in response, Dorothy blurted out, "Enough you two. Officer, Robert Ryan is a retired LAPD Detective who is not being very funny at this moment."

"Just didn't want to step on your toes Officer Kurtz." Ryan said with a smile.

"Sorry Detective, I had no way of knowing."

"It's quite all right Kurtz. I think the person responsible for this break-in is a guy named Richard Price, and right now he's on the FBI's most wanted list. I was about to call the Bureau

Chief to let him know his man is in town and looking for something he thinks I have."

"I'll call in and have the Lab people get on their way out here for fingerprints."

"Officer Kurtz. Is Teddy Boyle still with the Robbery Division?"

"Yes, Sgt. Boyle hasn't retired yet."

"When you call it in, tell him its Leo Metzger's house, we spent many a night playing poker here together."

Stepping off to the side, Ryan called the number the Bureau Chief gave him before leaving the office, and was put on hold for ten minutes before he was told, "Sir, may I have your number and I will have someone call you back in a few minutes?"

Ryan thought, shit, here we go again. "Ok, tell the Chief, Richard Price has come out of hiding, that will get his attention. My name is Robert Ryan and my number is 555-6969.

Five minutes passed and Ryan's phone started buzzing.

"Hello, Ryan here."

"Hello Ryan, its Agent Reynolds. What's up there?"

"Hello Barbara, how are you?"

"That's Agent Reynolds, Ryan."

"That's Mr. Ryan, Agent Reynolds."

"Ok, what's up Mr. Ryan?

"There was a break-in here at Mrs. Metzger's home and I think it was Richard Price's doing. The LAPD are here but I think you need to get back here if you're not too far away."

"So you're asking the bureau to get involved in a burglary?"

"Did the name Richard Price go over your head?"

"I'll be there after I speak with my supervisor, Ryan."

19

After talking with Ryan on her cell phone, Agent Reynolds exited the 405 Freeway, made a U turn and headed back to Woodland Hills to check out the break-in at Dorothy Metzger's house.

While everyone waited for the additional investigators to arrive, Dorothy went into the kitchen to make some coffee and see if she had some snacks she could put out for her unexpected company.

Within twenty minutes the neighborhood snoops who had come out of their homes to check out why the Metzger's home was surrounded by so many police cars, were lining up along the front fence.

Agent Reynolds had arrived back at the house and was just starting to question Ryan, when a very loud voice came from behind her asking, "Ryan, when the hell did you get back in town?"

Getting up from the recliner chair he was sitting in, Ryan said, "How the hell are you Tommy? I thought they would have put you out to pasture already."

"Two more years and I got my thirty in then I'm going out to do some Stud service on the farm."

Agent Reynolds decided she had heard enough and added her two cents, "If you two old war horses are done with your happy hellos, we have some business to attend to."

Ryan pointed at the agent and said, "Fed, what do they know."

After about an hour, the Fingerprint team had completed lifting dozens of prints from the rear doors of the house and the guest bedroom, but knowing whom they belonged to still had to be checked out.

Sgt. Boyle and Ryan had exchanged cell phone numbers and agreed to keep in touch. Agent Reynolds stood by Ryan in the guest bedroom as he started picking up his clothes and put them on the bed.

Picking up the book from the bed with fingerprint powder all over it, Ryan said with a smile, "I don't know when the hell I'm going to get time to finish reading this."

Ryan handed the book to Agent Reynolds when she asked to see it and she started thumbing through it flipping pages to the end.

As she flipped through the pages she said, "It's a shame you can't take time to finish this Ryan, it has a great ending."

Noticing that something was written on the final page, Agent Reynolds asked, "Is this your writing Ryan?"

Looking at the book as the agent turned it towards him, Ryan said, "Must be something my ex chief wrote before he gave it to me. What does it say?"

Studying it for a second or two she said, "What's behind the Black Da Vinci Code! Notice it doesn't have a question mark?"

"So?" Ryan said.

"I wonder what it means."

"Damn if I know."

"You told us the dead guy on the train put papers in this book, didn't you?"

"Yeah he did. So what's your point?"

Taking it back in his hands, Ryan slipped the red and gold cover off of the book and studied it for a second and threw it on the bed. Now holding the black book he noticed that the end binding behind the title was pulled away from the pages.

Holding the book cover out in a winged position, Ryan could see that something was tucked halfway into the binding.

Picking up a pencil from his belongings on the bed he pushed what appeared to be a black piece of paper out the opposite end into Agent Reynolds' open hand.

Looking at it briefly she said, "This is Microfilm, Ryan."

Slipping the small piece of film into an envelope provided by Dorothy Metzger, Agent Reynolds then made a call to her office to find out exactly how the Bureau Chief wanted to proceed.

Her instructions were to bring the item to the Lab for inspection to determine its contents.

Ryan told her, "Sorry to see you go Barbara, just when we were getting to know each other a little better. But you know what? Now it's out of my hands; just let me know what you find on that film."

20

Two weeks had gone by and not a word from the FBI, so after several phone calls that had not been returned, Ryan decided to take a trip to the Wilshire Blvd. office that morning. Although the Receptionist was very polite to him, he was told that the Bureau Chief was not available for a meeting with him but to leave a number where he could be reached.

When he asked to speak with Agent Reynolds, he was told that she was on assignment and could not be reached, again saying, "Please leave your number."

Trying to call the Agent on her cell phone had proved to be useless since the message said, "OUT OF SERVICE".

Looking through his wallet, Ryan remembered that he had the Bureau Chief's private cell phone number and made a call from outside the front door, since cell phone use is restricted in the FBI building. Once again Ryan's call was being ignored and he was starting to get pissed-off.

Driving back to the Valley the old retired detective passed many thoughts through his mind, most of which sounded like, "Screw the bastards--they wanted it; they got it. I'm done with all this bullshit. If they want anymore of my help they can kiss my ass to get it."

Stopping at the Denny's Restaurant on Ventura Blvd. to get a late breakfast, Ryan noticed a black Pontiac Firebird that pulled into the parking lot after him.

The car didn't mean anything special to him except reminding him of days gone by and a white Firebird he once owned that happened to be the same year.

Sitting at a window booth reading the menu, the observant ex-detective noticed that the driver of the black car didn't come into the diner.

Finishing his French-toast Slam breakfast meal, Ryan paid the cashier and headed for the parking lot. Noticing the Firebird was no longer in the lot he then got into his rented Ford and headed for home.

Before reaching Topanga Canyon Blvd., where he had to turn, Ryan turned into the parking lot of the Ralphs Market to pick up a few needed items.

After spending a half-hour and about sixty dollars, Ryan pushed his shopping cart slowly to his car bitching quietly about how much it cost to live today in California.

Carefully walking through the parking lot, he looked left and right making sure he didn't get his ass run over by some careless driver who might be talking on a cell phone or just stupid, he spotted something that caught his attention. It was then that he noticed that same black Pontiac Firebird about six spaces down from his car.

Because of the darkened side windows, it was impossible to see if the driver was in the front seat.

Thinking it could just be a coincidence; Ryan loaded the bags of groceries into his car and drove out onto Topanga Canyon Blvd. Instead of turning left on Burbank Blvd. he continued going straight for several blocks and turned into the large parking lot for the Macy's Department store at the Promenade Mall.

Parking near the front entrance Ryan walked into the store and watched through the glass doors as the Firebird passed by and parked two isles over, and once again no one exited the vehicle.

Walking through the store and exiting from one of the side doors out of sight of the Firebird,

Ryan circled around and came up behind the vehicle.

Opening the driver's door quickly he was surprised to see Agent Reynolds as she expressed equal surprise.

"Are we slumming Agent Reynolds, or just enjoying the beautiful qualities of the San Fernando Valley?"

"Very smart Ryan, what the hell are you doing?"

"Excuse me, what the hell am I doing? I'm minding my own damn business and you're following my ass all over the place."

"For some reason Ryan, Mr. Richard Price has developed a liking to you and has informed the Bureau that all communications with him will be done through you."

"That is horseshit Reynolds. I have not had any contact with that bastard and I don't care too."

"It's not your choice Ryan, it's his and I'm just staying close by so you don't screw it up."

"Screw it up? Screw you Reynolds and your whole friggen bureau."

"Like I said Ryan, it's not your choice, it's his."

"OK, let's get all this shit out in the open. What the hell is going on?"

"I'm not at liberty to discus that with you."

"Well then Reynolds, I'm not at liberty to co-operate with you, so good bye Agent."

"It's not that easy Mr. Ryan; there are some new problems with Richard Price that have surfaced."

"Well I'm sure that all the Pro's that you have at the Bureau can handle all of it without my help."

"That's where you're wrong Mr. Ryan."

"Reynolds, I don't know what all your crap is leading too, and I don't care, I have groceries to put away. So if you'll excuse me, I'm out of here. Bother me anymore, and I'll be contacting a lawyer."

"Bob, this is serious, we need you to co-operate."

"Bob, now it's Bob? No one in your whole bullshit organization has been straight with me, and now you want me to bend over backwards just a little more."

"I'll set up a meeting with the Bureau Chief and have him call you personally, will that help?"

"Right now a refrigerator for my groceries is all I need. Tell him to call me, but anymore crap and you people can deal with Price on your own."

21

Just as Agent Reynolds had promised, a meeting with Bureau Chief John Crane was set up for the following morning, and once again Ryan was standing in front of the receptionist at the Federal Building only this time he was immediately escorted to a conference room after a short ride on the elevator.

In the room seated at a long table were Agent Reynolds and three other people unknown to Ryan. The Bureau Chief was not in the room yet but was notified of Ryan's arrival and would be joining them very shortly, Ryan was told by the agent who escorted him.

Two of the people at the table talking to each other wore stick-on labels that read "VISITOR" and the third person, a woman, who had a name-tag that read "LAB" sat quietly and just stared at Ryan.

As Agent Reynolds started to introduce everyone, one of the men held up a finger to his lips and shook his head as if to say, "No, not yet."

Ryan looked at Agent Reynolds and asked, "What's the matter, did I forget my identifying code ring or something? I told you no more bullshit. Now what's going on here?"

Before Agent Reynolds could answer, one of the men looked at Ryan and said, "We are sorry Mr. Ryan, but everything will be explained in a few minutes when Chief Crane joins us. Please indulge us Sir."

Sitting down next to Agent Reynolds, Ryan decided to hold his tongue a little longer and see where this meeting of the minds was leading.

The quiet time lasted only a couple of minutes before Chief John Crane entered the room followed by another agent who remained standing by the door.

Taking his seat at the head of the table, the Chief asked Agent Reynolds to now make the introductions.

Agent Reynolds said, "Thank you Sir," and then, "Mr. Ryan, the gentleman to my left is Doctor Charles Bishop, who is an expert on exotic poisons and their effect on the human body. To his left is Doctor Harold Sawyer, an expert on Aquatic Marine life and deep-sea studies. Across the table is our own Doctor Marge Wilson, Senior Lab Technician and the West Coast's leading expert in the study of exotic poison control."

The Chief then said, "Mr. Ryan. The facts you hear at this meeting must remain confidential. If any part of what we discuss here gets out, it could be devastating. A diabolical maniac brought you into this mess that could result in very large numbers of lost lives, unless we stop him. You made it clear to Agent Reynolds that you would not co-operate unless you get the whole story. Well Sir, just so you know how critical this situation is, you are facing most likely the rest of your life in prison if you compromise this investigation in any way. Do I make myself completely clear?"

"Chief, first off, if you're going to sit there and threaten me with any of your bullshit you can count me out. Second, I didn't ask for this. I'm only here because I want to know exactly what is going on that keeps screwing up my life. And third, and most important, don't fucking threaten me or I walk out of here and you and all your experts can deal with all the shit. Do I make myself clear Sir?"

Looking at Ryan in a very cold stare, the Chief said, "For the record, I think we all have a complete understanding on both sides how important total co-operation and secrecy is to stop this threat to the nation."

Looking across the table and nodding his head as a signal to begin, the Chief said, "Doctor Sawyer."

Opening a folder in front of him that contained notes and photographs the doctor asked, "Mister Ryan, have you ever heard of a Sea Wasp?"

With a confused look on his face, Ryan answered, "A what? Did you say a sea what?"

"A Sea Wasp, Mr. Ryan, a type of jellyfish. It's known as Chironex, also known as Box Jellyfish."

"I can honestly say, doctor, that I have never heard of it. What does this have to do with Richard Price?"

"Bear with me please sir and it will all come together."

Doctor Bishop was the next to speak offering information about the chemical compound being formulated to supposedly attack and lower cholesterol in the human body, using plants that originally grew only in Africa.

"Mister Ryan, are you familiar with the plant life called, Septafsis Nitaris?"

Ryan smiled and answered, "No Doctor, that name does not ring a bell."

"It shouldn't Sir, it doesn't exist. It was just a name concocted by this Richard Price character."

Ryan asked, "But what about that formula that was being put together to help mankind with its cholesterol problem?"

The Chief spoke up, "It doesn't exist Ryan. It was just a hoax put out there by Price."

Looking confused, Ryan asked, "Then what the hell's going on?"

As the quiet fell over the meeting for a few seconds, it was then Doctor Marge Wilson's turn to voice a few facts. "Mister Ryan. The Sea Wasp or Box Jelly fish, whichever you want to call it, is the most venomous of all stinging marine life. It's usually found in Southeast Asian or Australian waters, but the poison has recently been identified in the LA City Morgue. Dr. Sawyer, would you like to take it from here?"

"As Dr. Wilson pointed out, the venom is extremely dangerous to all life forms. Although these creatures are not very large, they carry enough venom to kill several adults. The venom can cause death within 30 seconds, with respiratory paralysis, muscle spasm, and cardiac arrest.

Although an antivenin is available, in most cases the victim would be dead before the cause was diagnosed."

Dr. Wilson spoke up once again. "Mr. Ryan. It has been determined that a 55 gallon drum filled with the venom we are talking about could kill every person in California."

After sliding several pictures over to Ryan, Dr. Wilson said, "Chief, you want to take it from here?"

As Ryan studied several of the photos, Chief Crane stood up and slowly walked over to Ryan and placed a hand on his shoulder and said, "Price has informed us that he has over five-thousand gallons of the reproduced venom at a secret location and intends to use it at his discretion. The photos you're looking at are that of a village in Vietnam where a small amount of the artificial venom was added to the water supply. Of the one hundred and seventy villagers who lived there, one hundred and sixty three perished from the poison in a twenty-four hour period. Richard Price claims responsibility for the deaths."

Looking to the Chief for an answer, Ryan asked again, "So what does he want with me?"

"We don't know Ryan. All he said was that you would be getting further instructions and his intentions would be made clear."

22

Ryan sat in the conference room contemplating whether or not to co-operate with the FBI and be a go-between for them and Richard Price, he decided to use the situation to his advantage.

In a very insistent way, Ryan asked Agent Reynolds to pass him the blank pad and pen in front of her on the table, but before he started to write he said. "You want my co-operation, and that asshole Price says it's a must for negotiations. Well here are a few of my demands for my co-operation, and they are not negotiable."

Agent Reynolds asked, "What the hell do you want now Ryan?"

Bureau Chief Crane spoke up and said, "It's ok Reynolds, let's hear what he has to say."

"Thank you Chief."

As he started to write Ryan said, "First, I want my application for a California PI license approved and issued to me in the next few days."

Once again Agent Reynolds couldn't hold her tongue, "Ryan that takes time."

The Chief only had to look her way and hold up his index finger to his lips for her to quiet up.

"Next, I want my old gun permit renewed immediately, before I leave this room."

As he spoke Ryan wrote each demand on the pad.

"Third, I want Agent Reynolds assigned as a personal body guard at Dorothy Metzger's home for as long as it takes to capture or exterminate Richard Price."

Standing up and reacting to Ryan's demands, Agent Reynolds said, "Now you're going too far Ryan, I am no one's personal bodyguard."

Smiling just a little, Ryan responded, "It's not up to you Agent Reynolds, it's for your boss to decide."

Sitting back in his chair, Ryan asked, "What do you say Chief Crane, do we have a deal?"

Chief Crane said, "Get working on it Reynolds, all of it, please no back talk. We'll see what we can accomplish for Mr. Ryan."

"But Chief, I'm a Senior Agent not a baby sitter. This just isn't right, it's black mail and he knows it too."

Chief Crane looked at Ryan and asked, "Is that right Ryan? Are you black mailing the FBI?"

"I wouldn't think of it Chief. I only want to protect someone close to me who is no doubt in the sights of a madman who wants to use me, and will do anything to get it done. I also need my license and gun permit to protect myself and also open doors that would otherwise be closed to me. There's one other request you can add to my list."

Reynolds sarcastically said, "What's that Ryan, you want a personal body guard also, or a private jet or something elaborately ridiculous?"

"No sweetheart, I just want to be put on the payroll until this thing is over."

Chief Crane folded his arms across his chest and said, "Mr. Ryan, how about we get back to you tomorrow with our decision?"

"Chief, if I leave here without your decision, you guys can handle this madman on your own. I'll give you about thirty minutes. I noticed you have a cafeteria in the building from the sign I saw in the elevator and I could use a cup of coffee and maybe Danish, so you take a little time and come and get me when you've made your decision, how's that?"

Once again Agent Reynolds spoke her mind, "Be careful you don't choke on it Ryan."

The chief said, "You have something to do Agent Reynolds."

"I know you would be heart broken Reynolds."

"That's Agent Reynolds, Mr. Ryan."

"Be sure to put that on your nametag when you show up at Mrs. Metzger's home."

"Yeah, right Ryan. Like that's going to happen."

"That's Mr. Ryan to you sweetheart."

Standing up Chief Crane said, "That will be enough, Agent Reynolds."

Looking at Ryan the chief said, "Mr. Ryan, enjoy your coffee and someone will come down to the cafeteria with our decision."

23

Sitting in the cafeteria feeling smug and in control, Ryan sipped on his coffee and watched as patrons entered and exited.

Entering the cafeteria with a slight smile on her face, Agent Reynolds walked over to Ryan and said in a calm voice, "Mr. Ryan. Chief Crane and the Bureau have decided to take a different course of action in the case at hand. So Mr. Ryan, your services will not be required at this time. Don't let the door hit you in the ass Mr. Ryan."

"Quite alright Sweetheart, I've had my fill of this place. Give my regrets to the Chief."

Watching the agent walk away, Ryan decided it was time to head back to the valley and get on with his life, or so he thought.

The drive back to Woodland hills was uneventful with the exception of a phone call from a woman named Marie Bryant. Miss Bryant said she had information concerning Richard Price and needed to meet with him as soon as possible.

Pausing for a moment, Ryan referred her to the FBI. She came back with, "Patricia Gibbs sends her regards."

Taken by surprise Ryan asked, "Miss Bryant, what does Patricia Gibbs have to do with Richard Price?"

"I will call you again Detective Ryan."

Right in the middle of explaining that it is Mr. Ryan not Detective Ryan, she hung up.

Pulling over to the side of the road, Ryan tried to retrieve the caller's number but only got unknown caller for an ID.

Continuing on his drive home Ryan soon was pulling into the driveway and spotted an unfamiliar van parked in front of the garage.

Climbing the stairs slowly and cautiously, he then saw that the door to his apartment was open just a crack.

Standing to the side of the doorway he gently pushed the door open enough to see two women, one dusting and the other cleaning windows.

Letting out a sigh of relief, Ryan asked, "Who are you people."

Stopping her dusting for a minute she handed Ryan a card that read, "Rita's Cleaning Service." She then told him, "Mrs. Dorothy hire me to clean your rooms. Okay Mister Bob?"

"Okay Miss Rita, you keep working and I'll go see Mrs. Dorothy."

Walking in the back door to the Main house, Ryan found Dorothy in the kitchen washing dishes.

"Hello Robert, I thought I would surprise you by cleaning that place up. I hope the girls are doing a good job of it?"

"I wish you had told me first Dot; it could have gotten a little ugly."

"Well I couldn't expect you to live in all that mess, and besides it would have taken you weeks to clean up that place yourself."

Thinking of what to say next, Ryan just said thank you, and left it at that.

Dorothy asked, "How about a cup of coffee Robert?"

"Thanks Dot, that sounds good."

After pouring himself a cup of coffee, Ryan walked into the living room and sat down. He couldn't help thinking about the call from a woman he never heard of, telling him about Pat Gibbs who he met on the train from New Mexico who disappeared with Richard Price.

Right in the middle of his first sip of coffee, Ryan's cell phone started buzzing away and the caller ID said only, "BUSTER."

Continuing to let the phone ring five times he then answered, "Buster who?"

The caller responded, "Never mind Buster who. I don't like to be kept waiting, detective."

Recognizing the voice as Richard Price's, Ryan simply said, "Kiss my ass Price", and then hung up.

Only moments passed when the phone rang again. Once again Ryan read, "BUSTER."

Answering once again after the fifth ring, Ryan asked, "What do you want Price? I'm busy."

"So busy, detective, that you could stand by and watch people die?"

"For the last time Price, I'm no longer a detective, and you need to be talking with the FBI not me."

"Only you Mr. Ryan, only you, I will talk with only you."

"Look Price, I'm retired. My dealings with the LAPD and the FBI are over. I'm tired and this shit doesn't concern me anymore. You need to be talking with the proper authorities not me. Either give yourself up and stop this crazy mission you're on, or contact the people I've told you about. Now leave me alone."

Pushing the END button, Ryan then thought about what he had told the nut case, and then called Agent Reynolds.

The agent's response was, "Tell me everything that was said, and how did the conversation end?"

"Turn on your recorder Agent. I'm going to tell you this one time and then I'm done with it."

"From the sound of this conversation Ryan, he wants you involved and you are far from out."

"Reynolds, start recording or I'm just hanging up."

After a twenty minute conversation of questions and answers, Ryan did finally end the call but knew his involvement with Richard Price was far from over. Ryan did, however, renew his conditions and insisted they all be approved or his involvement is over.

24

One week had passed since Ryan's conversation with Richard Price, a time that was very productive for the once extremely active ex-detective.

Ryan first applied for his Private Investigator's License, which would take many weeks of background checks. The permit to carry a concealed weapon was much easier for him to obtain, considering his many years spent on the LAPD, and the help of the current police chief.

After a conversation with Dorothy Metzger, Ryan made a visit to the West Valley Animal Shelter, and after studying many of the dogs facing extermination, one in particular stood out.

Asking the Matron in charge if he could take the tan Lab mix in cage #6 out to the fenced-in grass area, Ryan knew in just a few minutes that he had found his new best friend and watchdog for Dorothy's property.

After signing the necessary papers and being instructed that the approximately two year old dog would have to go through a spaying operation, Ryan agreed and paid the adoption fee and was told he could pick her up in 48 hours.

Next stop was to a local auto dealership to purchase a used vehicle so he could turn in his rental car and stop racking up un-necessary expenses.

The purchase of a dark colored 4-door sedan seemed to fit right in with his personality, and all it needed was the shields on the doors and a light on the roof to make him feel like he had gone back in time.

The car dealer provided Ryan with a driver so he could return the rental and after dropping him off he returned home to inform Dorothy of the new found friend who would be joining them in a couple of days.

When she saw his new vehicle she smiled and said, "Looks like Detective Bob has returned home."

Ryan gave a smug smile and said, "Very funny Miss Dorothy, but no, Detective Bob Ryan is no more. It's Mr. Robert Ryan, Private Investigator."

"Okay Mister Ryan, there was a call for you while you were out, a woman named Pat Gibbs. She said she would call you back. She also told me it was very important that she talks to you as soon as possible."

"What else did she say Dot?"

"Is this someone you wish to tell me about Robert?"

"Just someone I met on the train and because of my wonderful personality I must have had a lasting effect on her."

"What a line of crap Robert, how about the truth now?"

Ryan said, "Just a woman on the train Dot, a woman who was taken away by some mad man who has a dislike for people, nothing more."

Dorothy put her hands on her hips and said, "You also had a call from an Agent Crane from the FBI who would like to speak with you. It seems there must be something wrong with your cell phone because you're not returning his calls. What's that about Robert?"

"I'll call him back, Dot, when I'm ready."

25

Sitting at his desk Bureau Chief Crane was reading a most disturbing report and when he finished going over the document he put his hand on his forehead and thought to himself, "why me?"

The report read as follows: "The Springs of Iosha received its name over five-hundred years ago according to tales told and remembered by the elders of the Eonka tribe in north-west New Mexico.

"Many centuries ago when the long brutal drought fell upon the area that the Eonka tribe had made their home, the daily ritual of the Holy man Shimako would be to pray to the heavens and Gods to bring water to the dying and thirsty people. Iosha, the young daughter of Shimako would sit each morning at the base of the mountain on the north of the village singing and praying in her own unusual way.

"One morning she moved several large stones between the boulders with the help of her brother Ticota giving her a shaded area to sit. As she sang and prayed that morning the ground surrounding her started to feel damp and within a short period of time a small puddle appeared. By nightfall water was flowing in a steady stream between the boulders.

"The word soon spread and members of the tribe gathered one by one until the entire village stood at the base of the mountain singing praises and bowing to Iosha.

"In reality, the young woman had uncovered a vein of an underground spring that traveled from the other side of the mountain out of a pool of collected rainwater now called Black Owl Reservoir. For hundreds of years, the water coming from the spring after filtering its way through the mountain was so pure and clean visitors would come to fill bottles daily to enjoy its fine taste and quality.

"Then one dark day, as if the Devil himself had invaded the spring, all who drank from it came down suddenly with an unidentified illness, which led to death within twenty-four hours until an antidote could be discovered.

"In all thirty-four people died of the mysterious illness, but the mystery was only to the local people and the medical profession, not to the FBI." The statement received by the Bureau the day after the antidote was discovered read, "How many more people must die before you meet my demands?"--- RP.

A copy of the statement went out to the Bureau Chiefs in the surrounding states. When an agent first brought a copy to Chief Crane and he read it he called for Agent Reynolds and a couple other senior officers to come into the office. When they all arrived he asked them, "Have I missed something here? What demands? That crazy man hasn't provided any demands. What is it that he wants?"

Of the three senior officers the only one not afraid to answer was Agent Reynolds who said,

"Sir, the only thing to date that Richard Price has asked for was that he wanted that idiot Ryan to handle all negotiations, if I'm not mistaking."

Thinking about what the agent had just said, the Chief instructed Agent Reynolds, "Contact Mr. Ryan and have him come in to see us."

Agent Reynolds protested, "But Sir."

"Now Reynolds, just do it and we'll talk about the consequences later."

While the Chief discussed the operation with the other agents in the room, Agent Reynolds left the room and returned to her office to use a landline to call Bob Ryan.

The conversation between the agent and Ryan lasted only a couple of minutes as she explained the Bureau's dilemma before the grumpy ex-detective said, "Goodbye Agent Reynolds, I told you this problem would come back to bite you in the ass. You passed on my deal when it was offered, now you can deal without me unless your boss has changed his mind. I'm still ready to negotiate but now I want a raise also and that's not negotiable."

Returning to the conference room, Agent Reynolds informed the Chief, "He refuses to co-operate Sir unless we meet all his demands, and now he says he even wants a raise and that's non-negotiable."

"Pick him up and bring him in here. Who the hell does he think he is? No wait. That's just what he would expect us to do. Let's go pay Mr. Ryan a visit and try to persuade him to help his government."

26

Ryan had named his new best friend Brandy, and she was an instant hit with Dorothy Metzger. So much so that after Ryan installed a doggie door in his apartment door, Dorothy asked him to install a similar entrance in her back porch door so Brandy could come and visit whenever she felt like it.

Time seemed to be whizzing by for Ryan. After all, it had only been six weeks since his arrival back in the Los Angeles area and so much had occurred in that time.

Ryan was becoming a real homebody, helping around the property with painting, gardening, and being an all-around good neighbor to the surrounding families.

While sitting in the back yard at the redwood picnic table reading the newspaper and enjoying a tall glass of iced tea with his dog Brandy by his side, Ryan seemed to be enjoying life to its fullest but it was short lived.

With a click of the front gate leading to the driveway, Brandy raised her head up from where she was lying and began barking.

Looking over the top edge of the newspaper Ryan watched as Bureau Chief John Crane and Agent Barbara Reynolds walked towards the table where Ryan was seated.

Brandy started to growl as they came closer until she was told by Ryan, "It's alright girl."
Lifting his paper back up, Ryan asked, "And to what do I owe this honor, Chief?"

"We need to talk Ryan and I thought you might be a little more comfortable having our conversation on your turf."

"What about you Agent Reynolds, do you feel more comfortable on my turf also?"

"Ryan, my own personal feelings are not an issue here. This visit is of greater importance."

Putting his paper down on the table, Ryan said, "All business today huh, agent, I like that, I think. Okay what's up Chief?"

Chief Crane sat on the bench opposite Ryan and started to explain his visit.

"The Bureau does not take lightly having to ask for assistance from outside help and having demands thrust at us. Because of the complicated issues involving Richard Price and his refusal to co-operate with anyone other than you, I am or should I say the Bureau is asking your assistance to capture or eliminate the threat he poses."

"I would be very happy to assist the Bureau in any way I can Chief, but…"

"But what Ryan"

"You know my conditions Chief and like I said before, it is non negotiable."

"Fill out the forms for your license and gun permit and get them to me."

"My application for a PI license has already been submitted. My request for a gun permit has also been submitted to LAPD pending approval. You need to speed up the process. As for being put on the payroll let's just say I will submit my bill for services rendered directly to your office for approval of payment each week. And Chief, let's make it retroactive from my first visit to the Federal building."

Chief Crane stared at him and said, "Seems like you have it all figured out Ryan?"

"Chief, either tell me now if we have a deal or not, or with all due respect, get the hell out of here and take your friend with you."

"Do you have copies of the forms you submitted?"

"Of course I do."

"Bring them to my office at your earliest convenience and I'll see what I can do to speed up the approval. As for you receiving payment for your services, just don't get ridiculous with your charges."

Looking at Agent Reynolds, Ryan said, "There is one more matter Chief."

Chief Crane stood up and stepped away from the table and said, "Agent Reynolds is far too valuable to be placed as a bodyguard Ryan. But I will assign a Junior Agent as soon as I return to my office. That's the way it has to be. And that's non negotiable."

Ryan smiled and said, "As long as he doesn't answer to Skippy and he understands that around here I call the shots, deal?"

"Fine Ryan, let's go Reynolds before he asks for his own parking space at the Federal Building."

27

The evening news on TV was just coming on when Ryan's phone started buzzing away. The caller ID read "unknown caller" but he answered anyway. "Hello, Ryan here."

"Well, Detective Ryan, are we enjoying a nice night in front of the TV or reading a good book on police etiquette?"

"Price, what the hell is it that you want? You made it clear to the FBI that you want all your bullshit negotiations to go through me, so what is it that you want? I'm listening."

"A little touchy there, detective, but I'm glad you're on board, now we can get something accomplished."

"Yeah, yeah spare me the crap, spell it out, and tell me once and for all what you want."

"I want you dead, detective. I want every memory of you erased. I want you to suffer. I want my face to be the last you see before you stop breathing. You Ryan, are the icing on the cake, the dessert after a fine meal, my swan song."

"You really are a nutcase aren't you Price? What the hell does your desire for my death have to do with you killing all those people?"

"Oh I have bigger things planned, but your death will be my bonus. Don't you understand detective? Does the name Prescott ring a bell with you or have you forgotten all about those fine people you were responsible for killing?"

"Yeah it does. They were some sick bastards who were killing innocent people years ago and I was fortunate enough to be involved with their extermination. Why do you ask? Were they your role models or something?"

There was silence for about ten seconds and then Price answered. "It's amazing how fate takes a hand in things, detective. You being a passenger on that train was more wonderful than I could have ever asked."

"I still don't get it you idiot. What's your connection to the Prescott's?"

Again it was silence for ten or fifteen seconds before he answered. "I paid that fat ass train porter to assign you to my compartment, you know, the Peters impersonator. He helped me in killing Stafford and then failed to complete his assignment to retrieve the lab reports. His early exit from the train was important to my plan succeeding."

"Look shithead, this conversation doesn't seem to be getting us anywhere, so unless you have something interesting for me, I'm going to just cut you off with have a nice day asshole."

Price said, "My, my, so vulgar detective."

"Yeah, with any luck I can have you joining the Prescott's very soon."

"I'm going to enjoy killing you Ryan, very slowly along with all who are close to you."

After saying, "Yeah, yeah call again," Ryan disconnected and immediately called Agent Reynolds.

The agent was not familiar with the case involving the Prescott family years ago, so Ryan gave her the short version of how a family of sick bastards killed off members of a jury who convicted Brandon and his brother William to prison on murder charges. Brandon received twenty years while William got the death penalty, but died in prison before he was executed. Justice was not served because William was an innocent man wrongfully convicted.

After being released from prison, Brandon, with the help of his sister, committed over a dozen murders to avenge William's death. Ex-Detective Robert Ryan was in Los Angeles investigating his ex-partner Leo Metzger's assumed suicide when he discovered Prescott's involvement.

Once it was revealed that Prescott was guilty of Leo's death, the LAPD used all of its resources to eventually track down the killer in Ventura, California.

Refusing to turn himself in after being surrounded in a little used abandoned medical facility; Prescott was shot and killed as he tried to escape.

The sister, Grace Davis, died at the hand of an off duty security guard in Portland, Oregon while she was attempting to take his life.

The agent asked, "So Ryan, what connection does Richard Price have to the Prescott family?"

"I don't know Reynolds, I couldn't get that out of him. That's why I'm calling you so you can get your people working on it."

"Did he give any other indication why he was poisoning all those other people?"

"Not at all Reynolds."

"How did the call end? Will he call you back?"

"I don't know. We'll have to wait and see."

"Okay, I'll inform the Chief of what you found out."

Ryan said sarcastically, "Okay Reynolds you stay in touch now."

"Yeah, good work Ryan."

28

Deciding to take a walk on the boulevard after having dinner with Dorothy, Ryan exited the property on the west side of the house next to the block wall that separated the property from the next-door neighbor's yard.

Although it's a poorly lit pathway, it has its own gate that is sometimes used by the gardener. Because of the heavy brush surrounding the gate, a person can come and go without attracting attention.

As he was about to open the gate, Ryan noticed a van parked on the other side of the street with two men seated inside who appeared to be on a stake-out.

Slowly and quietly Ryan crossed the street and walked right in front of the van, not appearing to notice its occupants, and continued walking east on Burbank Blvd.

Walking about a quarter mile, he then rounded the corner at Topanga Canyon Blvd. and ducked into an opening surrounded by hedges and stood there for a few minutes.

One of the men from the van came around the corner looking left and right as if he were trying to locate a lost or missing person. When he began to walk faster up the street, Ryan stepped out from behind the hedges and began following him at a quick pace.

As the man reached Ventura Blvd. he stopped and looked east and west and then removed his cell phone from his belt and proceeded to make a call.

Walking up behind him Ryan asked, "Are you lost Sir?"

Taken completely by surprise, the man identified himself as an agent and asked Ryan, "Why the hell can't you just co-operate?"

"Who the hell are you?"

"I'm Agent Chris Taylor, and I've been assigned as your body guard."

"You friggen twit. It's Dorothy Metzger you're supposed to guard, not me. Now get back to the house and keep an eye on Miss Metzger."

Ryan never noticed as he continued on his walk to Ventura Blvd that another pair of eyes had been watching every move he made.

Richard Price, who had disguised himself as a vagrant and was pushing a shopping cart filled with plastic bottles and aluminum cans, went from Dumpster to Dumpster all the time keeping an eye on Ryan.

A slow leisurely walk was exactly what Ryan needed to take his mind off all the bullshit that was cluttering up his life.

Looking in the store windows and watching the people who walked by he felt like a regular human being for a change.

By the time he reached Shoup Avenue, Ryan was starting to feel a little tired and decided to sit a while on the bus stop bench and rest his feet.

It was then that he noticed that the vagrant with the shopping cart had stayed fairly close and he started to get a little suspicious.

As he watched the man disappear into an alley next to a building, Ryan quickly got up from the bench and walked around the corner and hid in a parking structure waiting to see if he was being followed.

Richard Price, being much smarter than he was given credit for, did not fall into the same type of trap he witnessed the rookie FBI agent fall into only a short time before.

Suspecting that he was being watched and that Ryan was waiting for him to come around the corner following the supposedly unaware detective, Price crossed the busy boulevard and acted just like the down and out vagrant he portrayed.

As he stood in the shadows in the parking structure, Ryan watched, surprised that he had misjudged the poor old vagrant, but satisfied that he was not being followed.

Returning home, Ryan checked to see if all was fine with Dorothy Metzger.

With a slight smile on her face, Mrs. Metzger greeted him with, "I want to thank you Robert for sending me this fine young man", as she pointed to Agent Taylor seated on the couch.

"Taylor, what the hell are you doing in the house?"

Standing for a brief few seconds the agent said, "Just following your instructions detective."

Before Ryan could respond, Mrs. Metzger said, "Its okay Robert, I asked Agent Taylor to come inside after he came to the door and introduced himself. Please sit, Agent Taylor. You remain right where you're at."

"Dot, this man's job is to keep an eye on this house and protect you from harm. If he becomes too comfortable in doing that job, he could fail. I recommend he do his job from outside where he can watch and patrol the entire property."

"Robert, after Agent Taylor has a snack and a cup of coffee, and I ask him a few questions about his personal life, he can go back outside and patrol, as you put it."

"But Dot."

"No Robert, that's the way I would like it."

"Okay Dot."

Looking at the agent, Ryan said, "Taylor, nothing had better happen to this lady on your watch, or your ass is mine."

After that little speech, Ryan went out through the kitchen and walked to his apartment above the garage.

Turning on his stereo and tuning into a local jazz station he then sat in his corner easy-chair and then pulled out a book from the bookcase and started reading.

The book was "The Da Vinci Code" but Ryan could not remember where he had left off reading so long ago on the train ride.

As he flipped through the pages looking for something familiar, there was a knock on the door.

Getting up and walking to the door, Ryan slowly pushed aside the curtain and looked out the window and saw Agent Reynolds standing there with a bottle of wine in her hand.

Opening the door Ryan asked, "And to what do I owe this unexpected visit, Reynolds?"

Holding out the bottle she answered, "Peace offering Ryan, may I come in?"

"Sure, come on in and have a seat. All I have are paper cups if that will do?"

As Ryan placed only one cup on the table, Agent Reynolds asked, "What, am I drinking alone?"

"If you had done your home work on me Reynolds you would know that I don't drink alcohol at all, but I appreciate the gesture."

Getting himself a can of soda from the refrigerator Ryan joined her at the table.

"So like I said before, what do I owe this honor to?"

"Look Ryan, we got off on the wrong foot and I'm trying to correct that if you're open to it. If not I'll go and take my wine with me."

"Ok Barbara, truce.

The two touched paper cup to soda can and said, "To better days with better pay and no loss of life." An old police toast.

29

Agent Reynolds' visit to Ryan's home was not just a social visit; there was new information on Richard Price that she wanted to question him about and this seemed like the perfect time.

Checking into the background of the Prescott family, including Grace Davis, (the Prescott's sister) who was married to Anthony Davis, turned up a half brother named Richard Price.

After revealing the connection between Price and the Prescott's, Agent Reynolds sat back in her chair and asked, "Ok Ryan, fill in some of the blanks."

"What can I say that you probably don't already know?"

"Humor me, Ryan."

"Barbara, it would be easier to pull the old files on the Prescott family down at Parker Center. I had to give a complete statement before the case was officially closed."

"From what I remember reading, Ryan, you were in charge of the investigation and right up until the Prescott's were terminated. They had you in their gun sights. Is that about it?"

"Well that's the short version, but that pretty much says what they wanted for me."

"Did the LAPD or the DA ever investigate Grace's husband Anthony Davis?"

"At the time the investigation was in full force, Anthony Davis and Grace Davis were separated and Mr. Davis was in Mexico setting up a new business in Mexico City."

"Well the Bureau has done some checking on Mr. Davis and found out he died about three months ago while visiting a pharmaceutical company in Louisiana."

Ryan sat back in his chair and said, "Lot of shit connected here that's coming out about the nut-case Price."

"There's more. Anthony Davis was the controlling share holder in that Louisiana based pharmaceutical company and was about to sell off his shares and retire, under great duress from another large share holder, Richard Price."

"And what's going on with the company since the death of Mr. Davis?"

"From what the reports say, they're on the verge of marketing a new Cholesterol medication that will under sell all of its competitors and far out perform anything on the market today."

"That's nothing new. Look there are many new products coming out from what I've read."

"This new medication is said to reduce Cholesterol up to 75% and can be manufactured at a fraction of the cost of other products already on the market. This company intends to flood the market and wipe out its competitors with government assistance. "

"Very interesting and it sounds like a good reason to eliminate some of the share holders."

"The investigation has been underway for sometime now, but it's been stalled by some politicians he seems to have on his payroll."

"Barbara, by any chance have you been able to locate Patricia Gibbs?"

"It's an alias Ryan. Her real name is Beverly Andersen, but she seems to have fallen off the planet. By a real coincidence she was once employed by Price's company."

"Well if she happens to surface again, I'd like to have a long talk with her and now more than ever."

Agent Reynolds smiled, "Professional interest or personal?"

Ryan rubbed his chin and said, "With what you've just told me, professional."

"With that Ryan, I think I'll make my exit."

"Thank you Barbara for coming over tonight, on a personal and professional level. I really appreciated the peace offering of the wine, it was a nice touch."

"Not to take anything away from your wonderful thanks, but I had to come out and check on the rookie out there."

"Well you'll probably find him in the van across the street. I think he's a little pissed off at me for giving him shit about spending too much time in the house."

"Well Ryan, his job is to stay close to you. I'll check him out before I head on home."

Ryan smiled and said, "Let's do this again, huh?"

Getting up to leave and smiling, Agent Reynolds said, "I'll call you tomorrow if anything new comes up."

"Wait a minute and I'll walk you down to your car."

"That won't be necessary Ryan. I know the way, but thanks for the gesture."

Standing at the top of the stairs of his penthouse over the garage, Ryan watched as Agent

Reynolds walked out the driveway to her car parked in the street in front of the house. Walking back inside Ryan closed the door and proceeded to sit in his reading chair. Within seconds an enormous explosion that rattled the windows sent Ryan rushing to the door.

Agent Reynolds car was engulfed in flames and as Ryan ran down the stairs and towards the car he stopped short in his tracks when he saw that nothing could be done to save the woman who was obviously dead.

Calling 911 on his cell phone he reported the incident and then went to check on the young agent in the van who had not responded to the explosion.

When he reached the van, Ryan saw the rookie agent leaning over the steering wheel. Stuck in the back of his neck was a screwdriver, pushed all the way in to the handle.

This time Ryan called the private number he had for the Bureau Chief, John Crane. Filling the chief in Ryan was told, "I'll have a team of our people out there as soon as I can make the call. Watch yourself Ryan. You know Price is somewhere close so he can see the results of his fine work."

The first fire engine arrived before Ryan was off the phone with Chief Crane. Right behind it was the Paramedics ambulance, followed by the first LAPD patrol car.

The LAPD was soon to follow with four more black-and-white cruisers and two detective units.

By the time the fires were out, the Crime Scene Investigation unit had shown up, and as they started their work Ryan and a Detective Paul Crown went into Dorothy's house to go over his testimony.

There were about a hundred neighbors and spectators who had gathered so the decision to go inside away from the crowd was the best choice. Besides, Dorothy offered to put on a fresh pot of coffee. To Dorothy, coffee and pastry seemed to be just the right touch to calm any situation.

Before Ryan entered the main house, he stopped and stood on the front porch and turned to look at the burned out car and said silently, "Goodbye Barbara, rest easy, I'll find the bastard."

The strong silent ex-detective who usually was hard as concrete, had to wipe the wetness from the corners of his eyes.

As he closed the door and walked to the kitchen with Det. Crown, Ryan said, "Have a seat Crown, I'll try to fill you in on what's been going on."

30

All through the weeks following Agents Reynolds and Taylor's gruesome murders, there were so many questions and reports to be filled out.

The FBI increased the manpower they had searching for Richard Price and anyone else they felt were connected to the murder of the two agents. Ryan stayed in constant communication with the bureau but as the weeks went by there was no contact from Price.

An Agent Stephen Gibbons was assigned to help Ryan with his investigation and provided him with financial and employee information on the now closed-up pharmaceutical company in Louisiana. Agent Gibbons became Ryan's shadow and part time body guard with no complaints from the aging retired detective.

The pharmaceutical company had been under intense investigation by the FDA (Food and Drug Administration) for several years for suspected use of inferior ingredients in their products. Now with the disclosure of questionable ownership, a Federal order had been issued to close their doors immediately and all government assistance to end.

After a nice brisk walk with his dog on a Sunday night, Ryan returned to his apartment and found a letter taped to the door.

First looking around to see if he was being watched he then opened it cautiously and read the following, *"Hello Detective, it's been so long since our last talk. I hope all is well with you? I've been busy planning my next strategic move so I have been a little pre-occupied. It was a shame that the two agents had to give their lives, but we all have to make sacrifices. I will be in touch with you soon and provide you with a list of my demands. I will be watching you as I have in the past, but you'll never know it. Rest easy Detective, it's not your turn yet. R.P."*

After contacting Bureau Chief Crane, Ryan called his friend Chief of Detectives Ed Walton. Over the past few weeks, Chief Walton and Ryan had a couple of conversations about Ryan possibly re-joining the LAPD and using his experience to help the force in cold cases. After advising Chief Walton that he wished to follow up with the proper papers to make it so, Ryan felt a new surge of energy in his old bones. Although his memory was not as sharp as it once was, he felt he could contribute in many other ways to help the department.

Another call was coming in on his cell just as he was finishing up with the Chief and he could see from the caller ID that is was from the FBI office.

Agent Gibbons told Ryan, "Through diligent investigations the bureau has compiled information leading to several locations that Richard Price has called home. First there's a large compound in a secluded area in Louisiana not far from the now-closed pharmaceutical company. The location was his primary home while in that section of the country. While searching that location, a team of agents uncovered information leading them to three other homes used by Price as he moved around the country."

Ryan said, "Hold on Gibbons do I need to be writing all this shit down?"

"No need Ryan. I'll provide you with a full detailed list of all that I'm telling you. The interesting part of all this is, one of the homes was located only a few miles from Dorothy Metzger's home; it is located in a place called Calabasas, a way above average big money community."

"I know where Calabasas is Gibbons, what else do you have?"

Agent Gibbons went on, "A team of Agents is on the way to that location as we speak and an LAPD helicopter is watching all movement from the sky."

Ryan asked, "Has he been seen at that location recently, Gibbons?"

"One of the neighbor kids told an under-cover agent that Price was there last week, and there was a woman and another man with them."

"Could that woman be Beverly Andersen?"

"He didn't get a good description of the woman but the second man was a tall guy from what the kid said."

"Are there vehicles present at the scene?"

"A black Range Rover is parked in the driveway which makes us think that the house is occupied."

"What's the address Gibbons?"

"Look Ryan, you can't go charging in there and blow the whole operation."

"I'll wait for your call Gibbons, now what's the address?"

Ryan wrote down the address but was told again by Agent Gibbons not to approach the area until he notified him that all was clear.

That call came only ten minutes later from the agent but Ryan was already driving on the freeway headed towards the Calabasas location.

After the home was completely surrounded, but no contact was made with the occupants, several Agents entered from front and rear of the building.

Upon entering the home, a stench was immediately noticed and was unmistakably the smell of a rotting corpse.

Sitting up but tied to the chairs in the dining room were two people, one woman and a tall man, positioned in a way that their hands were on the table next to the plates laid out in front of them.

After the building was secured, Ryan entered and when shown the bodies positioned at the table he identified the woman as Beverly Andersen and the man, surprisingly, as Chris Heschel. Heschel was the third man who accompanied Ryan in his compartment on the train ride from New Mexico.

The connection now was very obvious that Richard Price had arranged for that compartment on the train and all of its occupants to be traveling together, and even more obvious that both of the men and Miss Andersen worked for him also in the charade on the train.

Studying the dining room table as the Crime Scene Investigators took pictures; Ryan noticed that there were six place settings, each with a name card.

At the head of the table there was Richard Price, then clockwise, Detective Ryan, Beverly Andersen, Peter Cole, Chris Heschel, and James Brace.

Cole and Brace were the unknowns, but sometime somewhere Ryan knew these people would turn up, most likely dead and thoroughly connected to Price.

In Richard Price's plate Ryan noticed a CD with the words "Play me Ryan" written on it with black marker.

Not wanting to disturb any of the evidence in the house, Ryan still picked up the CD and brought it to his car and played it with Agent Gibbons listening in from the passenger side of the vehicle.

The sarcastic voice of Richard Price came on in the first few seconds and said, *"Hello Detective Ryan. I'm sorry you didn't get the invitation to our little party in time but the invitations are going out for our next get together. It just wasn't your turn yet, detective, but your time will come. See you soon, your friend Richard."*

Ryan obviously upset said, "That son-of-a-bitch, he's enjoying this too much."

Agent Gibbons held the CD in his gloved hand after ejecting it from the CD player and said, "Ryan, we're going to dissect this house and with

145

any luck, maybe, just maybe, he left something that will bring us closer to him."

"He's too smart for that Gibbons. That bastard seems to know too much about what we do."

"He's going to slip up somewhere, they always do. His ego is gigantic so he knows no other way but to show us all how brilliant he really is. You know, a real psychotic."

31

Humphrey's Park maintains its snow caps about nine months a year and sometimes the white cold stuff stays around all year long and makes for some great skiing. Located in the mountains north of Flagstaff Arizona, the park is at an elevation of 12,630 feet making it the highest point in the entire state.

Trudy and Albert Wasserman visit the park two and some time three times a year to get in some vacation time with daily skiing. Conventional skiing and snowboarding has always been great fun in their eyes, but the exercise of cross-country skiing was a passion that they looked forward to with much excitement.

On the fourth day of a six day planned vacation while cross-country skiing about three miles out from the Peak Point Lodge, Trudy veered off to the right of the path most-traveled to look at a rock formation that had something reflecting the Sun light. As Albert called to her, Trudy continued towards the rocks keeping her eyes on the reflecting object. Stopping dead in her tracks, Trudy's screams echoed through the mountainside and quickly got Albert's attention. Hurrying to his wife's side he asked her franticly, "What's the matter Hon?"

Lifting her ski pole she pointed to the base of the large snow covered boulders and said, "Albert, look to the right of the middle boulder."

"Yeah, I see a branch sticking up."

"Look closer Albert. That branch has a wrist watch on it."

Sure enough, as they got closer to the large pile of rocks, it was obvious that it was a human arm sticking out of the snow, frozen in place with the rest of the body completely covered by the white surrounding blanket that was starting to melt.

Trying to call 911 on his cell phone, Albert found no signal available, so after studying the surroundings very carefully Trudy and Albert returned to the Lodge to inform the police of their findings. It took only thirty minutes for the local Sheriff to arrive at the Lodge and after a short ride on a couple of snowmobiles, the Sheriff and Albert arrived back at the rock formation. After a quick examination the Sheriff decided not to contaminate the crime scene any further and called in the findings to the Flagstaff FBI office. The decision to call the FBI was made after the Sheriff found ID on the stiff corpse. With much care he removed a billfold that read, "FBI: Agent Roland Holloway."

32

It was a Tuesday, six days since the discovery of Richard Price's home in Calabasas, and the two corpses tied at the table. Deciding to sleep in an hour or so longer on a cool rainy morning, Ryan was dreaming of hooking a thirty-pound halibut from a fishing pier he frequented often in his younger days. Finally winning the fight with the big beautiful fish he was already pan frying in his mind, he heard a buzzing coming from behind him that got louder as the seconds passed. Opening his eyes he realized that it was his phone that was buzzing away and he answered it with, "Hello, this better be important."

The caller was Agent Gibbons calling from the Federal building on Wilshire Blvd. and his information got Ryan to sit up quickly, "Would you repeat that, my mind was still out on Malibu Pier fishing for the big one."

"Agent Holloway's body was located by a couple of skiers on a snow covered mountain top just outside of Flagstaff, Ariz. It was found by a couple who were doing some cross country skiing, partially buried and frozen like a Popsicle."

"It was a positive ID Steve?"

"The skiers didn't want to touch the body and were smart enough to call the local Sheriff. He then contacted the Bureau and a team of our guys made the positive ID."

"They pick up any clues at the scene?"

"Nothing yet, but they're still working the surrounding area over."

"I know it's too much to ask for but, any papers, you know, documents on the body?"

"I don't have an answer for that Ryan."

"Had to ask."

"I got something else for you though."

"Whatcha got Steve?"

"My boss called your boss at LAPD and you have been temporarily assigned to the Bureau until this case is closed. What do you think about that Ryan?"

"Shit Steve. I didn't even know I had a boss yet. I've been waiting for a conformation from Chief Walton."

"Call Chief Walton this morning and then call me back. Oh, by the way Ryan. Chief Crane told me to let you know that your deal with him is officially over. You draw your pay from LAPD now. Call me back and I'll let you know what our plans for the day are."

Before calling Chief Walton, Ryan checked his cell and found six messages that he didn't know he had. Three of them were from Chief Walton.

It took about ten minutes to finally get the Chief on the phone and when he did finally answer he asked, "Been waiting long Ryan?"

"Only a few minutes Chief."

"Oh, I'm glad you weren't inconvenienced too long. I on the other hand have been waiting for you to call me back since yesterday. Where the hell have you been Ryan?"

"Sorry Chief, my cell was off and my mind was somewhere else."

"Well get all your shit together Ryan and report to Chief Crane at the Federal Building. You're on temporary assignment to the Bureau. Oh by the way, welcome back to the department, stop by and pick up your shield and service revolver."

"Thanks Chief, I know you went to bat for me."

"Another thing Ryan, watch your ass working with those Feds. They can be good guys or they can turn on you, just be careful."

33

For several weeks now the flock of attorneys representing the pharmaceutical company that Richard Price was the primary shareholder in, had filed an injunction to stop the closing.

Price, thinking ahead had already signed over all his shares in the corporation to the other shareholders for a cash settlement, so it was easy for him to just walk away from it all.

The Bureau had been calling in all informants who might have any information on Price or any of his connections to the Calabasas house.

The fingerprints found at the Calabasas residence revealed that a parole named James W. Brace had been present at the location at some time in the past. Mr. Brace was wanted by the

Cleveland, Ohio Police Dept. for questioning in the bombing of a local bar in that same town. The bombing resulted in the death of the owner and several customers.

Also through diligent work by the FBI investigation in Louisiana, it was discovered that a professional wheelman and chauffer named Leo Cole was in the employ of Mr. Price.

Richard Price knew that the only way he could get a little more breathing room was to hold better cards in the poker game he was playing with the FBI and the police.

Unfortunately it meant more people would have to die or at least face the threat of being exposed to a slow death. This was easy for Price because he had massive stockpiles of poisons around the country.

Ryan, who believed that Price was holed up somewhere in the San Fernando Valley, called Chief Walton and asked if it would be possible to get heavy press coverage with Price's picture plastered on the front page of the local papers. Also fliers printed up and passed out to gas stations, restaurants, fast food, and markets.

The Chief reminded Ryan that coverage like he was suggesting would be a great expense to the department.

Holding back his anger, Ryan asked, "And how much expense will it be to clean up all the dead bodies Chief?"

"That's uncalled for Ryan, and besides, I don't have the authority to approve a plan like that, but I'll make some calls."

Two days later, Chief Walton notified Ryan that his plan had been approved and the press and the TV news shows agreed to run pictures of Price in several different make-up scenarios.

It would be a couple more days before the fliers would be printed but the news shows were ready to run the pictures that night with the two major newspapers running the pictures the following morning.

A big break in the case came completely by coincidence with a phone call from an old woman who lived in North Hollywood.

A limo that had been parked in front of her house for three weeks was blocking her driveway, only by a couple of feet but it made it hard for her to swing into her drive each day when she returned home from work.

When the calls she made to the police were ignored she decided to call one of the local towing services that advertised instant response for removal of deserted vehicles.

After opening up the driver's door with a slim Jim tool, the driver noticed a foul smell in the vehicle and called the LAPD to investigate. Arriving at the scene, the police determined that the strong smell was coming from the trunk.

Deciding not to pry open the trunk the lead officer made the call that was needed and within twenty minutes there was an investigating team on the scene. Once the trunk was opened the body of a man in possibly his forties was discovered wrapped in a plastic drop cloth. With the FBI's help the identity of the man and cause of death was established in approximately twenty-four hours.

The cause of death was poison, the same poison that was being served up by Richard Price. The body was that of Leo Cole, the one time employee of Price who served as a driver and sometime bodyguard.

The limo turned out to be a cornucopia of fingerprints including Richard Price, Beverly Andersen, James Brace, Chris Heschel, and several unidentified people whom the Bureau was still looking into.

A canvassing of the area with house-to-house questioning of all the neighbors revealed nothing more than the officers already knew. The next step was to wait and see what the viewers and readers of the news would bring forth.

34

In an attempt to help locate Richard Price the FBI decided to work up a profile on him going back to his childhood with information found through public records and private records opened up by the Bureau.

Hoping to find something that led to the life he has chosen, the Bureau was surprised to find that Price had a very normal childhood. Price excelled in grammar school to the point where at the age of ten he skipped fifth grade and was placed in sixth grade because of his above average intelligence.

Price maintained a straight A grade average all through grammar school and high school.

After his acceptance at the Berkeley University of California, the extremely intelligent student improved to a 4.6 grade point average and received a Master's degree in economics and a bachelor's degree in Science Medicine.

Coming from good stock, his parents were Polish immigrants who both came to the United States as above average teenagers and went on to graduate from accredited colleges on the east coast.

Price lost both his parents one year after his graduation from Berkeley while traveling to the Bahamas. The private plane they were flying in went down and was never located.

For five years after the loss of his parents, Price went into seclusion and when he finally surfaced again he had become a very cold and bitter person with nothing but hatred and greed on his mind.

A marriage to a Miss Mildred Reese lasted only three years and produced one child, a son who died from crib death, and Price soon after divorced his wife who he felt was responsible.

Once again Price became a recluse, and was heard from only when he wished it, using disguises that he perfected as the years went on, establishing many identities with forged papers in different locations. He was known by several names and built a great wealth during this time.

With the extreme coverage by the press and the media and the $100,000 reward being offered for information leading to Price's arrest and conviction, after weeks of searching it was determined by the Bureau that the man had left the area. Each call and report of a sighting was investigated by the local police and the Bureau, but to no avail. Price, an excellent strategist, planned his moves carefully in the Valley and being a master of disguises was counting on the Bureau to look elsewhere for him.

Rather than hiding out in some sleazy hotel or motel, Price was heavily disguised as an overweight, gray-haired, bumbling Government EPA inspector on assignment to the west coast from Washington DC. Staying at one of the most expensive motor courts in the Valley, and having a private bungalow in the rear of the facility, it was easy to come and go as he wished.

A month had gone by with no contact from the wanted killer of so many people, when a break finally came. Although Price had instructed the management not to have cleaning personnel enter his bungalow without him being present, a new employee at the motor court did not understand the order and entered to do her daily duties.

Finding Price's make-up kit on the table was nothing to rouse suspicion, but several pictures of him in different stages of preparation caught her attention.

Los Angeles being a city where you can't throw a stone without hitting an actor or a wanna-be actor, the cleaning lady just figured that the occupant was one of those people.

While having lunch with several of her co-workers, Miss Maria mentioned the actor's belongings to her friend Connie who immediately told her, "No dear, he is a government man from Washington."

Miss Maria put her hands on her hips, "Okay, but why does he wear makeup and wigs to look like someone else?"

"Maybe he's a sneaky inspector and tries to fool people."

The two women just laughed it off and continued their conversation about other subjects.

Two days later the Daily News ran several pictures of Richard Price in different possible disguises and a caption, "Have you seen this man?"

While having her morning coffee, Miss Maria saw the pictures on the front page and knew she had seen that man, or at least seen pictures of him in that bungalow.

Calling the phone number in the newspaper, she first asked for someone who spoke Spanish. After Agent Carlos Ortega came on line, she reported what she had seen. Maria also explained that her greatest fear was that she was not a citizen or had a green card but knew it was the right thing to do.

The Agent she spoke with told her, "Ma'am, Maria, if this call results in the apprehension of the wanted man, Richard Price, the reward will help you gain your citizenship."

After recording the entire conversation, Agent Ortega told her not to say anything to anyone about what she had seen in the bungalow, or the conversation with him.

His other instructions to her were, "Go to work and do your job like nothing has changed and I will be sending a team of Agents to check out the tenant in the bungalow."

"Should I tell my boss?"

"No Maria, tell no-one. Do you understand? No-one."

35

Within two hours of Maria's call to the FBI, an advance team closed in slowly around the motor court on Ventura Blvd. in Studio City.

Posing as telephone repairmen, two agents approached the front door of bungalow #4. As one agent knocked on the door, the other stood at the ready with his service revolver clutched in his hand. After a minute of knocking and waiting for an answer the agents used a passkey to enter the unit.

Carefully checking the entire front room of the bungalow, the men slowly entered the bathroom. Stopping in their tracks they both saw the message written on the mirror in front of them.

First getting on his Nextel, Agent Rowe announced to other agents that all was clear. He then called in to Chief John Crane and read the message as it was printed, *"Did you think it would be that easy? RP."*

Without mentioning anything to the management of the motor court, Price had prepared his exit well in advance when he noticed that his bungalow had been entered without his permission.

Yes, Price was very smart in his exit. He even turned away security cameras in the courtyard, but not smart enough to notice one camera in the parking lot mounted on top of the building, which recorded many pictures of the vehicle Price was driving.

After viewing all of the security tapes of the past two weeks, a bulletin went out with the description and license plate number of Price's vehicle.

In the two weeks that followed, no sightings of the vehicle or Price were noted. Then while investigating a wild fire near Castaic Lake a vehicle at the center of the fire area was discovered on a remote dirt road. It was the vehicle Price had been driving.

Castaic Lake, situated approximately forty miles north of Los Angeles, gave the Bureau the idea that Price was headed north.

When Ryan was notified about the vehicle's location his response was, "I'll bet that the bastard planted the car there and headed the opposite way."

Although there were no reports of a stolen vehicle around Castaic Lake preceding or after the fire, it could only mean that Price hitched a ride south or he had an accomplice.

Because of Ryan's dealings with Price on the train ride from New Mexico, he felt that he had a better knowledge of the man's desires to carry out his outrageous plans for revenge.

36

Sean Danaher, a one-time vibrant redheaded Irishman who loved fishing on his boat almost more than life itself, sat in the Captain's chair on the flying bridge of his boat. The man sitting opposite him enjoying a beer in the sunshine was Richard Price. The two men had just completed a transaction that turned over ownership of Sean's boat, a 38-foot fishing boat with a large cabin that slept six and was fully contained for full time onboard living. Sean had owned the boat since its construction in the early eighties.

Mr. Danaher was suffering from a severe case of fast-moving intestinal cancer and had very little time left to tie up loose ends before his demise. Having had his boat for more than thirty years and docked at Marina del Rey, its access from Los Angeles was very easy for the fulltime or weekend fisherman.

Nine months remained on Mr. Danaher's docking lease and it was explained to Price that after the expiration the boat would have to be moved out for dock renovation. Price agreed on the terms and told Mr. Danaher that he would enjoy the solitude of living full time at the marina until the time came for him to leave.

After wishing the new owner good luck and many happy fishing trips, the teary-eyed Irishman left his beloved boat and started walking on the dock headed for dry land, occasionally looking back. Approaching a young man headed in the opposite direction, the slow-walking old fisherman stopped and said, "Good morning son, can I help you find someone?"

The young man said, "Looking for The Sea Chantey, old man."

"That was my boat son, I just sold it. Slip 14, just down there on your right."

"Thanks Pop."

Continuing down the dock the young man got to Slip 14 and jumped on to the deck of the boat saying, "Hello Mr. Taylor, nice boat you got here."

Using the fictitious name of Taylor, and hiring a vagrant off the street known only as Larry, Price felt his identity was safe as long as he continued using his disguise and didn't appear in public too often.

Prices' new means of transportation was an old blue Ford Station Wagon picked up in a cash sale at a super market parking lot, with no questions asked when cash does the talking.

After contacting one of his old most trusted lawyers, Tad Billings, Price was told repeatedly to turn himself in and face the charges.

The law firm of Pennton, Doyle, and Crenshaw, had been representing the Seebury Pharmaceutical Co. in Louisiana since all the trouble started, but was now throwing in the towel with the dissolution of the corporation.

Cash was never an issue for Price, it was something that he had plenty of and available to him no matter where he was in the world. Attorney Tad Billings loved the feel, smell and large quantities of new money he received from Price outside of the law firm. His decision to remain loyal to Price was a no-brainer to him considering his addiction to cocaine and women who liked the finer things in life.

Knowing that time was of the essence, the final plan for the torturous death of Ryan was being figured out, including the escape and disappearance of Price. The boat would be used as living quarters and then a means of escaping the area after carrying out his plans including Ryan's murder.

The stooge that Price hired to assist him, who just happened to resemble him in size and weight, would be blown up at sea during an unforeseen boating accident and to all interested parties Mr. Price would have gone out in a blaze of glory. In reality Price had plans to spend the rest of his life in the south of France with some cosmetic surgery to change his appearance permanently.

After making a couple of phone calls, Price sat his new crewman down and instructed him on what was expected of him and the chores he needed completed while he went into town for supplies.

Larry was also instructed not to leave the boat for any reason unless instructed in person by Price alone or his job would be terminated.

Adding a few touches to his disguise, Price drove to the Valley to spy on his favorite new target, hoping that Ryan was at home after a long day at the office.

It only took a short while driving north on the 405 freeway at 4pm for Price to realize that it was not a great time to be traveling on that road. As bad as it was he was even more depressed when he turned onto the Ventura freeway headed west and the traffic was at a standstill.

A trip that should have taken possibly forty-five minutes was already in its second hour because of accidents on both roadways. Not having things his way and having to bend or conform to conditions he had no control of was not acceptable to Price.

It was 6:30 PM when Price parked his vehicle in front of the apartment building directly across the street from Ryan's residence. Disguised to look like a man in his eighties, Price exited the car and slowly walked down the street appearing like a lost soul searching for some address.

Working late night hours had become very common for Ryan and by the time he got home most nights he was dog tired and turned in early. Richard Price had been watching and studying Ryan's movements closely and was preparing a surprise for the tired detective.

37

Almost two months had gone by without any contact or sighting of Richard Price. The FBI and LAPD had not backed off one bit on the search for the madman, but it seemed like he just disappeared as he did once before, only to surface after some mass killings.

Ryan was being used more and more back at the LAPD on other cold cases. His thoughts never let him forget that there was a crazed killer out there who promised to end his life and the lives of many others in a horrible and painful way. Ryan also knew that anyone in his company or close to him was also in danger.

The possibility of being watched and studied by Price was something that Ryan was aware of, or at least expected and down deep inside he felt it, but could never spot the bastard who had him in his sights.

The legal eagles of the FBI and the Food and Drug Administration had been dissecting all the known files of the pharmaceutical company, and through the diligent work of one young man something new was discovered.

While checking thousands of notes on experiments made in the pharmaceutical lab, the young rookie investigator noticed some eraser marks of penciled-in notations.

Using equipment designed especially for this type of discovery, Agent Patrick Dillon revealed several interesting statements. One scribble read, "Never overlook the obvious." Another, "#937 antidote only temp." Also, "#1436 true blue complete dilution of test poison #67, carry always while in presence of #67." The notes were those of John Stafford, the man who died on the train.

When all of the experiments were examined it was found that no record of experiment #1436 existed or of #67. There was no mention of it in written records, computer files, or notes of any kind. It appeared that all findings of #1436 and #67 died with Mr. Stafford on that train.

A request for all of John Stafford's personal belongings was issued and everything was brought in boxes to the Federal building for a thorough investigation.

Spread out on the floor of the large conference room was everything retrieved from the man's apartment, office, storage facility, and bank safety deposit box.

With so many sets of eyes checking every stitch of the man's personal belongings you would think that something would show up related to #1436, but nothing.

Even the obvious medicine cabinet in the bathroom held nothing out of the ordinary, containing only band aids, iodine, aspirin, Chap Stick, after-shave lotion, anti-perspirant and shaving cream.

Kitchen cabinets were almost bare considering that John Stafford spent very little time in his apartment in Oxnard.

His residence in Louisiana was also torn apart and dissected looking for information on #1436, but there too nothing was found but normal home furnishings and items found in any home across the country.

All the belongings removed from Stafford when his body was searched on the train were sent to the Bureau and inventoried and stored for safekeeping. They were all laid out on the table and consisted of: a wallet, address book, keys, loose change, a nasal inhaler, aspirin, a ballpoint pen, a watch, pinky-ring, and a thin gold chain that he wore around his neck.

Parked in the garage at his apartment was Stafford's only vehicle, a 2000 Cadillac STS, but other than his golf clubs and golf shoes, the trunk was empty.

Dumping out everything from the golf bag revealed nothing that the everyday golfer wouldn't carry with him, like tees, balls, gloves, pencils, aspirin, and spare change. It was starting to appear that #1436 was something that either was completely eliminated or never existed at all.

38

Lying in bed listening to a little light jazz playing on his clock radio, Ryan also heard the plunk, plunk of the raindrops on his roof.

Being a Sunday morning and the prediction on the weather for the day was bleak with the Sun hiding behind the rain clouds, the tired old detective decided to rest his bones a little longer. Not getting home until after midnight because of a retirement party he attended for an old friend, he was beat.

Rolling over between the sheets as he rubbed his head and then scratched at his groin, Ryan felt like he was lying in a bed of itching powder. All of a sudden the bites started that felt like pins sticking him in his legs, his ass, and his back.

Scratching and rubbing at his body he threw the covers back and turned on the light next to his bed. Not believing his eyes he saw dozens of small brown spiders crawling on his legs, sheets, and blanket.

Jumping up and grabbing a newspaper from the table, he started swatting at the little critters for a few minutes until he became dizzy and had a hard time standing.

Just barely remaining conscious, he pushed 911 on his cell phone and asked for help, then fell to the floor.

When Ryan awoke, he had needles with tubes attached stuck in both arms and the sound of beeping coming from the monitors next to the hospital bed he was lying in.

His new surroundings were in the Encino/Tarzana Hospital and he had no idea how long he had been there.

Using the assistance call button that was hooked on the railing of the bed, Ryan pushed it a couple of times and then closed his eyes again.

When the nurse came in she said, "Well good morning Mr. Ryan, welcome back."

"How long have I been here?"

Looking at his chart the nurse said, "You were admitted to Emergency about forty-eight hours ago, transferred to the ICU poison control ward three hours later, and that's where you are now."

"Two nights, I've been here two nights?"

"Yes. According to Toxicology, the poison that entered your system could not be controlled by your immune system and the allergic reaction almost killed you."

"Poison, what poison?"

"Let me get the doctor Mr. Ryan and he can give you all the particulars."

Still groggy, Ryan asked, "Wait a minute please. What poison?"

"From what I understand Mr. Ryan, you were bitten numerous times by extremely venomous spiders. You went into anaphylactic shock and lost consciousness."

"Spiders, you mean those little shit ass bugs did this to ne?"

"Yes. Now let me get Doctor Noble, and he will answer all your questions"

Ryan tried to sit up but fell back. "One more thing nurse. How did I get here?"

"Paramedics, Mr. Ryan, from a 911 call. Now rest, I'll be right back with the doctor."

Closing his eyes and weighing out all that he had just heard from the nurse, Ryan was slightly startled by, "How are we feeling Det. Ryan?"

"We? From what I've heard, we are glad to be alive."

Doctor Stephen Noble, short in stature but big in the ego department, started naming off all his credentials concerning toxins when Ryan interrupted him and said, "Okay Doc, you can fill me in on all your accomplishments later. What kind of damn spider could do this to me?"

"Okay detective, we'll cut to the chase. It's still early in our final determination but the Crime Lab is leaning towards the Brown Recluse Spider, but unless you have something in your make-up that makes you extremely allergic, the Recluse Spider should not have had this type of reaction on an adult. The amount of spiders in your bed however could result in the death of a small child."

"How the hell can a spider bite do this?"

The doctor folded his arms across his chest and said, "Spider bite detective, from what we've found on your body, you were bitten approximately fifty times, and your Lab boys rounded up about twenty-five of those little brown critters, some alive and some dead."

"My apartment must have been infested and I must have somehow upset a nest of the little bastards."

"The FBI Crime Lab is involved also and they are expediting information from the National Poison Control Center, and we hope to have more information on the spiders very soon."

"When can I get out of here Doc?"

"For now just rest up detective, you are going to be our guest for a while longer. You may think you can stand and walk but take my word for it, your legs probably won't hold you up very long. I'll keep you informed as the new information comes in, lie back and rest."

"Thanks Doc. Oh one more question. Can you unhook me from this crap so I can get up and at least take a pee in the toilet instead of leaking into that plastic bag on the side of the bed?"

"For now detective, we need to keep the catheter in place but maybe in a few hours I'll give the order to remove it. You may think you're strong enough to walk, but trust me, you're not."

"I'll tell you what doc, you win this one, but I can't stay here to long. I have a job to get back to."

"Detective, the nurse will be in here in a few minutes with some oral medication. Cooperate with her, rest a while longer, and we'll get you out of here as soon as we can. How's that?'

"You got a deal, doc."

39

When the toxicology reports came in on the venom that had entered Ryan's body from the spider bites, Dr. Noble along with FBI Lab technician Dr. Fred Snyder and Officer Christina Kurtz of the CSI department at LAPD, all converged in Ryan's hospital room to fill him in.

As Doctor Noble had promised earlier, Ryan had been disconnected from all the tubes and the catheter and was sitting up in bed when all his visitors entered the room.

After all the introductions were made Dr. Noble took the lead. "Detective Ryan, according to the Ag Center at LSU Entomologist Department in Louisiana, those little brown critters that you were sleeping with were Brown Widow Spiders. Its venom is more toxic than the Black Widow's, and their bite only gives off about half as much compared to it's black relative, but at ten times the potency."

Lying there with a look of disbelief on his face, Ryan asked, "So where the hell did they come from?"

Dr. Snyder answered first. "Detective, those spiders were imported from Louisiana. They are not known to live outside of tropical areas, and Louisiana at this time appears to be the most common place to find them."

"So how the hell did they wind up in my bed?"

Officer Kurtz took that question to be more directed at her and said, "Det. Ryan, your bed was sabotaged. At the foot of your bed, between the sheets we found a gel like sack that had contained the spiders and under the warming conditions from your body heat, the sack dissolved and released the venomous intruders."

As Ryan relaxed his neck muscles and laid his head back into his pillow, the only thought he had circling his mind was Richard Price.

Ryan looked at Dr. Noble and asked. "How soon can I get out of here Doc?"

"The good news, detective, we now have the proper antidote for the poison. The bad news is that we will have to keep you here until we see what kind of reaction you have to it."

Ryan asked, "How much longer doctor?"

Dr. Noble said, "Twenty-four hours, no more."

Ryan thought for a few seconds and realized that arguing would be futile, so he asked Dr. Snyder if he would please relay all the information to Bureau Chief Crane at the FBI. He next asked Officer Kurtz if she would do the same and notify Chief Walton at LAPD.

Ryan added, "When you speak to your superiors tell them Richard Price has surfaced again and is responsible for this. They will understand."

Dr. Noble spoke up, "detective, it's time for you to rest. You will receive an injection of the antidote. Dr. Snyder, Officer Kurtz, the detective needs to rest. You can continue this meeting tomorrow if you wish, but for now, everyone out please."

40

The first of two injections had just been administered to Ryan and with the room lights dimmed a bit he started drifting off into dreamland when his bedside phone rang.

Answering with a groggy, "Hello", the caller said, "Hello Detective, long time no talk."

Not recognizing the caller's voice, Ryan said with an annoyed, "Shit, who is it", before the light in his brain clicked on and he pushed the call button for the nurse.

"I'm hurt Detective. Our train ride meant nothing to you, but so much to me."

Ryan had written on his note pad, "Nurse get the FBI agent or the LAPD detective back in here quick, Richard Price is on the phone."

While waiting for someone to get back into the room, Ryan started talking about anything that came into his mind babbling on about nothing. When questioned by Price about his ramblings Ryan said, "It's the drugs I'm on Price. Give me a minute to clear my head."

Chief Walton and Chief Crane had still been in the hall talking when the nurse showed them Ryan's note.

As soon as both men reentered the room, Ryan yelled into the phone, "Price, what the hell do you want, haven't you caused enough trouble. Isn't it time you give your self up?"

"You do remember me. Now I'm happy again. No Ryan, that's not going to ever happen, I enjoy causing you trouble. Now tell me how bad you feel. I need to get that warm fuzzy feeling hearing about your pain."

"Price you bastard, some day we are going to meet eye to eye again and I'm going to kill you. Do you hear me you bastard?"

"Does that mean you didn't like my little brown friends?"

"If I get my hands around your throat, I'll show you how much I appreciate your little stunt."

"I'll come to see you one night detective, and you can show me just how much you really care. For now, I have to say good bye."

Frustrated that he could do nothing, Ryan slammed the phone receiver down and cursed quietly when Price disconnected the call. Ryan asked both Chiefs, "Did our people find out where that call came from?"

Chief Crane said, "All your calls coming in are automatically being traced Ryan. Give me a few minutes and I'll let you know where it came from."

After making a phone call, Chief Crane put the receiver down and said, "The call was made from an un-traceable throw-away cell phone. Our man Price is covering his tracks quite well."

Once everyone left the room Ryan laid his head back on the pillow and within minutes was into a deep sleep. Several hours had passed when Ryan was gently awakened by the presence of Chief Walton and Dorothy Metzger having a conversation a few feet from his bed.

Speaking in a low voice, Ryan asked, "I hope you brought me something good to eat like a hamburger or a sub sandwich Dot?"

Dorothy smiled and asked, "How are you feeling Robert?"

"Much better now Dot, but I can't wait to get out of this place."

"Hello Ryan, you look like you're enjoying your time off?"

"Hello Chief, any news on Price?"

Sitting down on one of the chairs he had pulled over to the bed for him and Dorothy Metzger, Chief Walton said, "Not a word from him, but we know he's out there watching this hospital so we're going to get you out of here under cover of darkness tonight."

"What time is it now Chief?"

"Its 6 PM Ryan, if you haven't noticed, you're not connected to the machines any longer with all those tubes and the doc say's you can leave at any time. So we're going to get out of here and let you get dressed so we can get you the hell out of here."

Ryan said, "You know that Son-of-a-bitch just called to harass me and tell me he was going to pay me a visit. It's all bullshit chief."

"And what did you tell him Ryan?"

"I told the bastard I wanted to get my hands around his throat and choke him to death."

Dorothy said, "Robert, that's not like you to act so unprofessional."

"Dot, you have no idea what this man has put me through and what he's capable of."

"Robert, I had the exterminators out to the house, and they not only did your apartment, but the main house also. I had a house cleaning service then come out and clean up everything, so all is ready for you to come home."

"Thank you Dot, I'm looking forward to sleeping in my own bed."

Chief Walton said, "Ryan, you know if Price contacts you again you need to find out all you can about his location. He'll find out real quick that you left here today, so we had your home phone set up with a trace on it. You know the drill; keep him on the line as long as you can."

"He's shown us that he's smarter than that chief, but who knows, even the best slip up at some point. Now, when do I get out of here?"

"In just a few hours. We're making the arrangements."

The move from the hospital during the night was handled in a very smooth way with Ryan leaving through an employees entrance at the rear of the building dressed in doctors scrubs and walking with a couple of nurses trying not to draw any attention. Taking the precautions not to be followed, they eventually wound up in Woodland Hills at Ryan's garage apartment after driving many surface streets.

41

A little over three weeks had gone by and Ryan appeared well rested and fully recovered from his episode with the little brown spiders. It was a pleasant sunshiny late afternoon and Ryan sat eating a juicy hamburger in his favorite eatery, Mel's Diner in Sherman Oaks about ten miles east of his home on Ventura Blvd. As he watched people walking by wondering what it would be like to lead a simple and normal life, he munched away on his burger and just enjoyed the view. Ryan loved sitting in one of the booths by the front windows looking out on Ventura Boulevard, watching traffic go by as he ate.

Stopping for the traffic light, two buses back to back blocked the view for a few minutes. Studying the people who were riding on the first bus, the Metro Local, Ryan counted six women and three men just out of habit. On the second bus, the Metro Express, he counted nine men and two women.

The passengers on the buses had no real significance, but as the metro vehicles pulled away and Ryan once again had a clear view of the Pavilion's Super Market parking lot across the street, someone caught his attention.

He hadn't noticed the vehicle earlier, but sitting in an old Ford LTD station wagon at the left side of the lot, the driver was looking towards the diner through a pair of binoculars.

Thinking he might just be a little paranoid, Ryan went back to nibbling away at his French fries and reading his mystery novel that he always brought with him when he ate out by himself.

Occasionally looking up he noticed that the person in the LTD hadn't moved and was still sitting there and seemed to be observing the diner.

Approximately an hour had gone by and Ryan's curiosity was starting to get the better of him. With all the coffee he had consumed he needed to use the rest room and he had a plan brewing in his head to check out the Ford wagon.

The waiter, David, nicknamed Double D, came over to the booth and topped off Ryan's coffee cup for about the fifth time, and Ryan asked him if it would be all right for him to exit the rear of the building through the kitchen to do some snooping of someone he felt was spying on him.

With a big smile and a, "Anything you need my friend is okay with me." Ryan then headed for the men's room to first take a leak and then sneak out the back door through the kitchen.

Ryan had left his book and jacket in plain sight in the booth when he took off for the John. After pushing the bath room door open, he ducked down and made his way into the kitchen.

Borrowing David's baseball cap and jacket from a hook by the back door, Ryan crossed Kester Avenue that runs along the east side of Mel's, and walked down to Ventura Blvd. and crossed the street. Never looking toward the LTD, Ryan headed straight for the market.

Walking in the entrance Ryan quickly turned and looked out of the window and saw that the car was still there. Walking out of the exit he headed straight for the LTD with his 9mm held down at his side.

Ryan was still about fifty yards away when he heard the engine cranking and then saw a puff of smoke come out of the tailpipe. Within a couple of seconds the big station wagon was backing up right in his direction extremely fast.

Jumping to his left to avoid being run over, Ryan looked up from the ground and saw the face of the driver before tumbling to his side.

Richard Price smiled as he sped out of the parking lot side swiping a fairly new Cadillac that happened to be entering the lot. Ryan fired two shots at the rear window shattering it but Price never slowed down.

Laying down his weapon Ryan pulled out a note pad and pen from his shirt pocket and wrote down the license plate number and a description of the Ford LTD station wagon.

The faded blue paint with its wood decaled sides to make it look like a woody was fairly common on the older LTD wagons, but the severely damaged right rear quarter panel and rear door gave it a marking that was distinctive.

As a few people gathered around him one woman asked, "Are you alright sir?"

Ryan answered, "I'm fine Ma'am I'm a police officer, thank you. Is anyone hurt in the Cadillac?"

"No, but the old woman in the passenger seat is a little shook up."

Getting up from the ground and brushing himself off, Ryan picked up his gun, holstered it and took out his cell phone calling in the description of the vehicle and license plate number to one of the detectives in his division at Parker Center.

Walking with a bit of a limp, Ryan walked back across the street to Mel's, where he was greeted by Double D standing in the doorway who asked. "You didn't get a chance to lock his ass up huh?"

"No, but I got a good look at the bastard."

Double D. said, "Let me get you a fresh cup of coffee my friend."

Sitting back down in the booth, Ryan took out his cell phone again and made a few calls. The first call was to his buddy Art Wilson at LAPD, Auto theft division in Van Nuys. Det. Wilson took down all the information and told him he would call him back in about a half hour.

The second call was to Chief Ed Walton and filled him in on what had just happened. The Chief wanted a full report on the incident, which Ryan told him he would provide first thing in the morning at the Police Administration Building (PAB), the new home of the LAPD since leaving Parker Center.

The third call was to Dorothy Metzger to ask her what year Leo's old green Ford station wagon was that he had when he joined the force back in the seventies.

The familiar look of the wagon reminded Ryan of his old partner's beat up old Ford that they rode in so many times on under cover stakeouts.

Dorothy told him, "Robert, I'm not sure, but I think it was a 1971 Ford LTD Wagon, but again, I'm not positive."

While calling Art Wilson back to informed him of the year of the station wagon, Ryan watched as two black and white patrol cars pulled up in the lot across the street. He told his friend Art about the severe damage on the vehicle and asked him to check if anything fitting the description may have been involved in an accident.

Sgt. Wilson told Ryan he would need more time but he would get back to him if not tonight, tomorrow morning after checking with DMV.

Walking back across the street to fill the officer's in, Ryan showed his ID and informed them that he had already talked with the Chief and would be filling out his report as soon as he returned to the PAB.

Back in the diner, Ryan thanked his friend David, sat back and enjoyed his cup of coffee and then took a nice slow and easy drive home, looking forward to a soak in the tub to ease the pain of his newly acquired bruises.

42

The, "Be on the lookout" report with the vehicle's description went out right away, but even with so many police and highway patrol looking for his vehicle, somehow Price was able to elude them on the thirty-five mile trip back to his boat.

Very angry with himself for being spotted by Ryan in the parking lot of the super market, Richard Price sat on a folding chair on the deck of his boat just staring out at the bay in Marina del Rey contemplating his next move.

Price's on-board helper, Larry, brought up a scotch and water for his boss and a beer for himself. Larry then asked, "What's troubling you Mr. Taylor?"

Keeping his calm Price said, "Nothing much Larry, just thinking about a little trip I want to take with the boat in a couple of weeks. We may need to hire one more deck hand for the trip. Do you know someone with some boating experience?"

"I know a guy I met in the mission downtown who could use the money. He told me once he used to go fishing a lot when he was younger back in New York."

"Does he have any family out here?"

"Nah. He divorced his wife years ago and she went back to the east coast."

"White guy, black guy, Hispanic?"

"He's a white guy, around my age."

"Get a hold of him tomorrow, I'd like to meet him."

"Sure, no problem Mr. Taylor, I'll try to find him tomorrow."

"One other thing Larry. I need you to get rid of the old shit-box station wagon I've been driving and find me a nice van."

"How much do you want to spend sir?"

"Four or five thousand should cover it I think. Oh, and pull those license plates off the wagon before you dump it."

"Dump it sir?"

"Yes Larry. It's a piece of shit and I don't want anyone else to get stuck with it."

"Why the plates sir?"

"They actually don't belong on that car. They came from another car at the super market. Just remove them and bring them back with you or toss them down a sewer after you purchase a van. It will make the wagon harder to trace."

After going down to his cabin and returning with an envelope filled with cash, Price handed it to Larry and said, "Something not too showy. Maybe white or tan."

"You trust me to take this money and buy a truck Mr. Taylor?"

"Of course Larry. If you let me down or disappeared with my money, I hope you know that I would hunt you down, torture you, and then kill you. So I trust you will do the right thing."

"You can count on me Mr. Taylor."

"Something else Larry. It's time you knew. My name is not Taylor, its Price and I'm being hunted by the authorities. For now that's all you need to know. I hope that doesn't change things between us Larry, because I need to be able to trust you completely?"

"No sir Mr. Price. What ever you need sir, I'm your man, you can count on me to keep your secret."

"I knew I could count on you Larry. Now go take care of business."

43

Det. Art Wilson left a message for Ryan to call him when he arrived at work that next morning, informing him of a lead on the vehicle he was looking for.

Wasting no time, Ryan hauled ass up to his friend's office stopping only at the hallway coffee machine for his morning fix of caffeine.

After a quick greeting, Ryan asked, "So what do you have for me Arty?"

"First thing is those plates are not registered to a Ford station wagon, they belong on a 1981 Toyota Celica. The owner of the Toyota reported them stolen two months ago after she noticed them missing and believed they were taken while she was parked in a super market lot in Marina del Rey."

"What about the wagon?"

"Hold on cowboy I'll get to it. A station wagon fitting the description was involved in a hit and run in Venice a year ago, and the damage to the vehicle was similar to what you described, but the partial we had on the plates didn't match. We also came up with several parking tickets that were issued and never taken care of while the wagon was parked in the metered lot at Marina del Rey and the plates didn't match."

"Arty, we need to get a couple of cars over to the marina and discretely investigate."

"Way ahead of you Ryan. As a matter of fact, the vehicle was spotted about a half hour ago leaving the parking lot at the marina and at last report was driving east on Washington Blvd."

Staying out of sight as much as possible, the LAPD black and white cruiser dropped back even farther when the undercover sedan took over following the blue station wagon.

Pulling into the parking lot of a Home Depot Center, Larry found a parking space at the extreme left of the lot and parked. He then locked the vehicle and entered the store.

Not knowing with certainty that he was being followed, but being street wise and very careful, he took all the precautions he felt necessary to complete his mission for his boss.

Walking quickly to the rear of the building, the soon-to-be elusive assistant of Richard Price exited the store through the receiving area and disappeared from sight.

Larry knew exactly where he was going as he made his way through the back alley and over the block wall to a narrow little street that led to the Red Line Subway Station.

Purchasing a ticket from the machine and keeping out of sight for several minutes he soon hopped aboard the train that would take him to Union Station, in downtown LA.

By the time the LAPD had their helicopter in place over the Home Depot store, Larry was safely on his way to meet up with his old friend at the Downtown Mission.

When Ryan heard the news that the driver of the station wagon had eluded the police surveillance, he was furious. He had already contacted the FBI and informed them that the investigation was progressing smoothly and hopes of locating Richard Price was very likely. Ryan did let them know that there seemed to be some kind of link to Marina del Rey and he hoped that they also saw some connection.

Once it was confirmed that the driver was nowhere to be found, a team was sent to the Home

Depot lot to examine the vehicle. It would then be towed to an LAPD location for a complete check for fingerprints and anything else that might lead to the capture of Price and his accomplice.

Once again a chance to locate Price was wasted because of poor methods and Ryan was not pleased at all. When he called Chief Crane and voiced his disappointment with the bureau he was told, "Trust me Ryan, it won't happen again."

44

It was around 9:45 AM when Larry walked through the front doors of the Los Angeles Mission. His friend Greg was easy to spot standing by a very large industrial coffee maker. The dozen or so other people in the room were all seated except for Greg and an old woman who was called Simple Sally. Larry knew Sally from his days living at this God-sent place and as he walked closer she smiled at him with the few teeth she had left.

Although Sally didn't have the sweet smell of the very expensive perfume she once used in her more fruitful days, Larry hugged her and told her she was as beautiful as ever and handed her a folded up twenty dollar bill he had taken from his pocket.

After shaking Greg's hand Larry filled a cup with coffee and told his friend he needed to talk with him in private.

Sitting down at a table in the corner where they could talk without being overheard, Larry explained to Greg about the job that was available to him, without disclosing anything about his boss or his identity.

The only problem Larry could foresee was Greg's problem with drinking, but his friend assured him that he would control the urge. He said, "Hey buddy, I got seven days sober as we speak, I'm on a roll."

Greg wasn't living at the Mission, even though he spent most of his time there, helping with clean-ups and taking out the trash after each meal, earning free meals and gallons of coffee.

Greg wasn't always a lush. After graduating high school he spent nine months trying to find out where he fit in society and decided he didn't, so he joined the Army to be all that he could be. After serving his country for twenty-one years he called it quits at the age of forty, with a pension that he would receive for the rest of his life.

Unfortunately, without working that monthly check could only buy him a month-to-month bed and locker in a local flophouse near the mission, and the booze he needed to keep his glow in place with a touch of food now and then for strength.

With his new found sobriety and the job that Larry was offering, Greg told his friend, "Hey Buddy, this could be my ticket out of this hole I dug myself into."

Larry explained how he needed to find a van for his boss, and he was prepared to purchase it immediately and then return to Marina del Rey.

Greg suggested several places that he knew that had vans he thought for sale, but Larry told him, "No, you don't understand. I need to buy a van out-right. Cash. No paper work except the title and the cash change hands, and then we drive away, period."

Saying "Let me think about it for a while." Greg got up from the table and got two more cups of coffee and when he returned he told Larry, "Lets go down the street to the 76 station and talk to Wally."

"Who's Wally?" Larry asked.

"He works at the gas station and I bet he knows someone with a van for sale."

45

With his pasted on beard, clipped on ponytail, sun glasses and an LA Dodgers baseball cap, Richard Price was able to walk around the Marina undetected as the madman wanted by the police and FBI.

Walking to the food mart just on the outskirts of the Marina was a jaunt Price had taken many times, always paying close attention to his surroundings. On this particular morning Price noticed many more people roaming around the parking lots stopping some of the regulars and questioning them.

As bold as could be, he walked up to one of them and asked, "Hey, what's going on?"

After being shown a photo of a blue 1971 Ford LTD Station Wagon, and an artist's sketch of Price himself, he was then asked, "Do you remember seeing this vehicle parked in one of the lots here, or the man in this sketch?"

Studying the two pictures and stroking his beard lightly, Price asked, "Who is he and what did he do?"

The response by the non-observant undercover officer dressed in jeans and a T-shirt was, "I'm sorry sir, I'm not able to talk about the person in question."

"Let me get this straight. Officer is it? You can't tell me who it is, or what he's done, but you want me to help you locate him?"

"That's right sir."

"Well I'm sorry I can't help you. I don't recall seeing that car or that man around here, but I'll keep my eyes open."

As the officer handed his card to Price, he said, "If you do see him, don't approach him, just call the number on the card and report the sighting."

Shaking his hand, Price then walked away smiling and thinking to himself, "What an idiot."

Price knew time was running out and it was also time to move on and leave Marina del Rey as soon as possible.

46

When Larry and Greg walked into the 76 gas station, Greg looked for the mechanic he had known and had coffee with many nights while keeping him company in the shop.

The cashier in the convenience store told the men that Wally would be back in about a half hour. She also asked if there was anything she could help them with.

Greg was familiar with the woman and told her they were interested in buying a van if Wally had one or knew of one for sale.

Seeing and talking with many of the customers, she told them of a company just down the street that had a for sale sign on one of their trucks that comes in for gas every few days and gave them the address.

Deciding to hang around the station for the half hour and wait for Wally, they were surprised when he returned early and confirmed that the van down the street was a great buy for the $4,000.00 they were asking for it.

Larry asked, "Do you think they're sticklers for paperwork or can we do an, all cash deal with no paperwork involved?"

Wally thought for a few seconds and asked, "And who are you?

"I'm sorry I'm Larry, Greg's friend."

Wally said, "Let me give the owner a call and see if I can feel him out about the paper work."

After a quick conversation on the phone, Wally told the guys, "George will be here in a few minutes with the van and you can make your offer. Oh, by the way. I'm sure he'll take around $3,500.00 if you hold out the money in front of him."

Sure enough, about fifteen minutes later a light blue Chevy van with a FOR SALE by OWNER sign on it, pulled into the station and parked in front of one of the bays.

A short balding guy about sixty, smoking a twelve inch cigar and looking a lot like Danny Devito on the old TV show TAXI, got out and walked over to Wally and shook his hand.

Wally introduced Greg and Larry and said, "Now be nice to these guys George, they just want to give you money."

After a quick look at the van and pointing out a few small dents here and there, Larry made his pitch. "George, Wally told us the van runs ok, but looking at it close I can see it needs a shit load of tender love and care. The sign says $4,000.00. What's the best you can do for a quick cash sale? No bullshit?"

Taking a puff on the "goat shit" smelling cigar he was smoking, George scratched the bald spot on his head and asked, "What are you offering, in cash that is?"

Using a slow pause, Larry took out the envelope from his pocket and thumbed through the pile of hundred dollar bills in plain sight of George and said with a smile, "My first offer is $3,000.00. I have to fix a bunch of dents."

Again scratching his bald spot and puffing away on his cigar, George countered, "So leave some of the dents where they are and give me $3,500.00."

Larry removed his ball cap, scratched his head and said, "Throw in one of those cigars and you got a deal, mister."

George told Larry, "Follow me down to my shop and I'll get you the title for the truck and a cigar. Listen, you hit anybody or anything and the police come looking for me, I'll swear that you stole the truck and the ownership papers were in the glove compartment and you forged my signature."

Larry told him, "All I need is the Pink slip George, you know, the title. You get the money, I get the van and I'm gone, no other paper work. If I get stopped I'll tell them that I ripped off the truck, deal?"

After another scratch and puff, George said, "Deal."

The walk to George's business took only a few minutes and the whole exchange of money and title took about the same. As George handed Larry the van title and two cigars, he said, "Remember, you have any accidents and I swear you stole the fucking truck, capeesh?"

Larry not knowing what George said, agreed, "Capeesh."

47

Driving back to the marina in the newly acquired van, Larry and Greg joked about how they both seemed to have fallen into the best job they had ever had.

Pulling into a large strip-mall, Larry spotted a pick-up truck off to the side and parked next to it. As Greg stood lookout, Larry stepped out of the van and removed the license plates from the pick-up with his pocketknife screwdriver.

After the license plate theft the two men drove down the road about a mile and stopped at a food market and picked up supplies for their voyage at sea. The food supplies and other articles that were on a list Larry carried in his pocket were purchased at a couple different stores, before the men headed back to the boat.

The trip back to the marina took only forty-five minutes and after putting away the supplies the two crew members sat back in deck chairs and enjoyed some liquid refreshment, Larry a beer and Greg a Coke.

Approximately twenty minutes went by when Richard Price stepped down off the dock onto the deck of the boat. An introduction, followed by a line of questioning by Price went on for several minutes before the new member of the crew was told, "You'll do just fine Greg. Remember, whatever you see or hear on this boat is private information. You tell anyone what goes on here and I won't just fire you. I'll put a bullet in your head and dump your body overboard about fifty miles out to sea with an anchor tied to your ass. Is that clear?"

Greg looked at Larry who just put his hands in the air and then said, "That's very clear sir."

48

Ryan was sitting at his desk at home going through a pile of mail he hadn't bothered to open for several days, when he received a phone call from FBI Agent Bonnie Tyler who had recently been assigned to the Richard Price case.

Agent Tyler wanted to meet with Ryan to pick his brain a little about Price, possibly finding out more about the man and information not being in the official records.

Ryan told her, "I can make my self available anytime you want to talk."

A surprised response to his statement was, "How about this evening Det. Ryan? It just so happens that looking at my appointment calendar I'm free for the night."

Since it was only 7 PM and Ryan was getting a little hungry he said, "Tell you what Tyler, I haven't eaten dinner yet tonight and if you hadn't called I would probably just snack on cookies, crackers, or some other crap I have on the counter."

A slight chuckle was followed by, "Oh, a man after my own heart. Chief Crane told me you and I had a lot in common but I thought he might be joking."

"How is the Chief, we haven't talked in a while? Oh never mind. We can talk about him later. Are you familiar with the Valley, Tyler?"

"Born and raised in Sherman Oaks, and its Agent Tyler. So where do we eat Det. Ryan?"

"First off, Agent Tyler, you can just call me Ryan, I don't answer too much else. How's Denny's work for you?"

"Fine Ryan it's a date. How about telling me which one?"

"Ventura Blvd., across from Taft High School. Meet you there in about an hour."

"Sounds good to me Ryan. Ask them to make a fresh pot of coffee. I can't stand old stale coffee."

Ryan laughed and said, "How about that. You're a woman after *my* own heart."

Arriving at Denny's ten minutes early and expecting the Agent to be much later than the agreed time, Ryan was surprised as he walked into the restaurant and was greeted by a woman sitting in the first booth on the left.

"Hello Ryan, right on time."

"Do we know each other Miss?"

"That's it, Copper, make a date with a girl and pretend you don't know her."

With a surprised look on his face followed by a smile Ryan asked, "Agent Tyler?"

"In the flesh."

After shaking hands and sitting down, Ryan noticed a scent of perfume that warmed and excited his libido and asked, "Well first off Agent Tyler, what is that heavenly perfume you're wearing?"

Smiling with a slight blush, the agent said, "It's a personal blend of gardenia and chypre, I use it to lure men to my way of thinking."

"Well you sure got my attention Agent….."

Stopped mid-sentence the agent said, "Hold it Ryan, I have a feeling you and I are going to be spending a lot of time together, so please, call me Bonnie. There's a time and place for all the formal crap, and this isn't it, ok?"

With the biggest smile on his face since he was a kid in a candy store, Ryan held out his hand again and said, "I like you already Bonnie."

As she pushed a file across the table and asked about a few things that didn't seem to make any sense, Ryan just stared at her not listening to her words. Studying his new friend's casual dress and lack of make up he thought to himself, "What a beautiful woman. Dark brown hair, green eyes and by no means a skinny stick figure. Possibly fifty years old, tall and maybe a hundred and fifty pounds, I think I'm in love."

Noticing Ryan's lack of interest in what she was saying, the agent asked, "Are you listening to me Ryan, or am I talking to the wind?"

"How tall are you Bonnie?"

"How tall am I?"

"Yeah. How tall are you?"

"In heels or bare feet?"

"Standing on your head. How tall are you?"

"I'm five eight. Do you want to know my weight too?"

"No, I already guessed that at around one fifty."

"I'm 157 in the buff. You want my age too?"

"Nah, I figure you're between 45 and 50 but you look more like 40."

"Well thank you all to hell kind sir, I'm 51. Is there anything else of my private life I can tell you?"

"I'll probably come up with a few more questions but for now, oh yeah do you always follow proper bureau procedure?"

"What the hell kind of question is that?"

"Do you always do what you're told by your bosses, yes or no?"

"No, but I'll deny I ever said it."

"Bonnie, do you remember the last line in 'Casablanca?'"

She looked at him for a few seconds in deep thought and said, "Louie, I think this is the beginning of a beautiful friendship. Close enough?"

"Damn near word for word. I'll tell you what, ask me anything sweetheart, I'm yours for the taking."

After enjoying an absolutely wonderful evening with Agent Tyler, and trading information about the elusive Richard Price, Ryan got back home around midnight with new hope on catching the bastard that had made his life miserable since they first met on the train.

49

With the new member of his crew in check, Price laid out charts of the local waters and the coastal charts of the Northwest and proceeded to plot the trip that would start in just a couple of days.

The FBI and the LAPD, un-be-known to Price had started collecting security videotapes in the area surrounding Marina del Rey, with the hopes of spotting the old Ford LTD Station wagon and its driver.

After viewing hundreds of videotapes of security cameras all around the marina and surrounding stores, a break finally came. A young woman officer who was burning the midnight oil spotted the LTD in the background at a Marina food mart store on a two-month-old security tape.

Careful studying of the videotape with blow-ups, close-ups, and image enhancing, proved unquestionably that it was Price's car.

An additional twenty tapes were viewed and the LTD showed up in the Marina parking lot near the restrooms and showers next to Basin H. However, the man who drove the vehicle away after using the facility the last time was not Price.

Four Agents of the FBI worked overtime viewing over a hundred videos until they too spotted the vehicle at different locations.

With a detailed map of the entire marina, the agents marked locations the vehicle had been parked, and with the information provided by the LAPD, the area in question tightened and a plan for a boat-to-boat search would soon be in operation.

50

It was 5:15 AM on a Sunday morning and with all intentions of sleeping late it proved not to be the case for the tired detective. Cursing away, Ryan was being rattled up out of a sound sleep by his phone buzzing away on the nightstand. The caller ID read, B. Tyler.

"Good morning Ryan, let's go fishing."

"Are you crazy lady, its 6 AM?"

"Got a lead on Price, he's living somewhere in Marina del Rey."

"Is there a team going or is it just you and me on a stake out?"

"Let's just say we're going fishing, so don't wear your detective clothes this morning. You know something that a fisherman would wear."

"And what will you be wearing Miss Tyler?"

"Jeans and a sweatshirt."

"So what do we do for poles and fishing gear?"

"I have everything we need in my trunk."

"You mean you fish too?"

"Hey Ryan, does a bear poop in the woods? Come on get the hell out of bed and I'll buy you breakfast down at the marina."

"Be still my heart. Tell me you like John Coltane, Miles Davis, and anything that comes under the heading of Jazz and blues and I think I'm in love."

"What about Monk, Charlie Parker, and Muddy Waters?"

"Okay, enough foreplay. When do you want me to be ready for our first date?"

"Ryan, if you look out your front window, I'll wave to you I'm parked in your driveway. Get dressed so we can get some coffee and get on our way."

Getting dressed in record time, Ryan was walking down his steps when he was greeted by Dorothy Metzger in her jogging sweats.

"Good morning Robert, where are you off to so early on a Sunday morning?"

"Believe it or not Dot, I'm going fishing."

"And is that pretty woman parked in the driveway your fishing partner?"

"You don't miss a thing, do you Dot?"

"I've been up for an hour already Robert, took the dog for a walk around the block, took a little jog, and when I returned she was parked right in front of the driveway. She's a pretty one Robert, don't screw it up."

"Actually Dot we're going to check out a lead on a suspect we've been after for a long time."

"Do you need any fishing gear, because Leo had several poles and boxes of fishing gear in the storage shed?"

"Thank you Dot, my partner came well prepared."

"Please be careful Robert."

"Hopefully we'll reel in a whopper."

51

At the same time Ryan was greeting his new fishing buddy, Richard Price was meeting with a man named Eldred Wisco at 'The Café Driftwood at the marina.

Still using the name James Taylor, Price had made arrangements to meet with Mr. Wisco to rent the man's fifty-foot sailboat one week earlier for a very large fee all in cash.

As the final rental agreement was being signed over coffee and donuts, Price placed a large manila envelope on the table, smiling and saying, "Who knows Eldred, if I like it, I may make you an offer you can't refuse to buy your little baby. Maybe a big enough offer that you could buy yourself a much larger boat."

"Mr. Taylor, James is it? You'll find that you will have your hands full with my little sailboat, but when you return from your trip we can talk. For now, let's see what you brought me in that envelope"

Sitting in a secluded booth in the rear of the restaurant it was easy for Mr. Wisco to open the envelope and dump out its contents on the table. As he flipped through each of the ten packs of hundred dollar bills, each containing ten thousand dollars, he smiled and said, "Best kind of payment, tax free."

Price, with a serious look on his face said, "Just remember Wisco, part of that is a security deposit and I'll expect that returned if there is no purchase deal in the making."

"And you remember this Taylor, thirty days. After that you forfeit your deposit and I call the police."

"For some un-foreseen reason that I am delayed, you will be notified well in advance, and amply compensated. Please notice that I added that to our contract."

Looking over the typed contract on the table Wisco spotted the additional clause that was penned in by Price and said as he crossed it out, "Thirty days Taylor, no exceptions, understood?"

"You made yourself clear Wisco. You'll see me again in thirty days."

52

As he whistled and walked down the driveway towards the front gate Ryan was pleasantly surprised to see Agent Tyler sitting behind the wheel of a Forest green 1967 Chevy Malibu SS convertible.

As he got in the passenger side he asked, "Is this Bureau issue, or did you borrow it from The Petersen Auto Museum?"

"Well good morning to you too Ryan."

"And good morning to you Miss Bonnie."

"If you must know about the car, and I'm sure you're going to bug me until I tell you, six years ago I hit the Lottery for a few thousand. I gave my Mom and Dad ten thousand and bought the car of my dreams with the rest."

"How's it run? Does it have any balls?"

"I'll show you once we get on the freeway. Buckle-up now. I don't want you to get a ticket."

"Okay Speedy, let's go catch some fish, or the bad guy's if we can hook em."

As the Agent put the shift lever of the four-speed transmission in first gear, she smiled and pulled away from the driveway making a u-turn and headed for the freeway.

With few cars on the road at that time of the morning, it was easy to show off a little without over doing it. In one quick burst of power the agent floored the gas pedal and pinned Ryan to the back of his seat.

When Ryan asked, "What's under the hood lady?" She said with a smile, "396 V-8 375 horsepower and it's all mine whenever I need it."

It took a little over a half-hour to get to Marina del Rey, and a few extra minutes to decide where they would go for breakfast.

Since they were near Mindanao Way, they decided on The Café Driftwood.

Parking in the lot across from the popular early morning eatery, Ryan and Tyler walked slowly to the Café front door. Unaware they were being watched from inside of the diner, they smiled and talked as they entered choosing to sit at one of the booths with a view of Basin H and the beautiful boats tied up in their slips.

The eyes watching their every move were those of Richard Price who had stopped at the diner for coffee.

As the pair of newly arrived visitors sat and ordered their breakfast, Price suspected that their arrival was more than a coincidence.

The plan that Price had put together for his smooth exit from the area would now be changed. The new plan would incorporate the abduction and death of Ryan and his new partner far out in the Pacific somewhere.

Walking swiftly to his boat, Price told his two deckhands, Larry and Greg to follow him back to the diner and explained a plan to kidnap Ryan and his female sidekick.

Pointing out the couple as they sat sipping coffee after eating, Price then returned to the boat to wait for and prepare a big surprise for his guests.

53

With the taste of a wonderful breakfast still fresh on their palates, Ryan and Tyler walked to the end of Mindanao Way to look at the sights from Burton Chase Park, with a clear view across the main channel of the marina.

When Tyler told Ryan of a plan that involved walking up and down each basin dock to observe the residents who appeared to live at the marina, Ryan asked, "And where's our back-up?"

Tyler said, "They're on the way Ryan, but let's get our gear and take a walk."

With a floppy hat, sunglasses, and a fishing pole in hand, Ryan figured they could walk along un-noticed and fit right in with the surroundings.

Before their plan could be put into action, a man approached them who asked, "Are you looking for a guy named Price by any chance?"

Immediately surprised and suspicious of a stranger offering information on Price, Ryan asked, "Who the hell are you?"

"My name is Larry, and I worked for the man you're looking for, and I can take you to him."

"And why would you all of a sudden decide to turn on your employer and take us to him, as you say?"

"Because he screwed me over and he owes me money that he refuses to pay."

After a quick glance at Tyler, Ryan asked this new provider of information, "And where do you intend to take us?"

"Just to the other side of the marina. Price lives on his boat at one of the more quiet docks."

"Is he by himself, or does he have other people around him?"

Pointing at his associate Greg, who had been standing about twenty-five feet away next to a palm tree, Larry said, "We are the last of his help and we can't stand the bastard."

"Ok Larry, so how do we get there?"

"Well, we need a ride. It's too far to walk around to the other side."

As they all walked back to Tyler's car, Ryan asked. "So Larry, how did you know who we were?"

"That's easy Detective. Price has your picture pinned on the wall of the cabin right next to the cabin door. So every time we leave the boat we see your face."

After they all loaded into Tyler's car, she asked and followed directions to the parking lot on the other side of the marina. Parking near the walkway leading to the docks, Tyler shut off the engine and turned around to face Larry who was now pointing a gun right dead in her face.

Ryan, who had been looking out the side window, turned his head towards the rear seat as Tyler tapped him on his knee and said, "Surprise."

In a very calm voice, Larry said, "I will blow her fucking face right off if you try anything Detective."

"Ok Sport, What do you want?"

"Both of you. Slowly remove your guns and hand them to my friend here. Like I said, slowly or she is dead."

As Greg took control of both handguns that were handed over the seat, Larry told his friend, "Take the safety off one of those and keep it pointed right at her head."

After removing a small case from his shirt pocket, Larry told Ryan, "Stretch your left arm over the back of the seat and keep looking forward."

Pushing Ryan's sleeve up past his elbow, Larry injected him with something that quickly rendered him unconscious.

Seeing what had happened and knowing that she was next, Tyler tried squirming in her seat and explaining how interfering with the FBI was a crime that would surely put both men in prison for a long time.

Larry's response was, "Yeah sweetheart, we know. Now hang your arm over the seat, or die here because we don't need to bring you with us."

Within only a few minutes, Ryan and Tyler were being carried to Price's boat, and it was actually closer to the boat ramp than Ryan had been told.

When Price saw the men struggling to carry Ryan down the walkway, he came to help. Tyler was much easier to carry and when all were aboard the engines were started, ropes untied, power lines unplugged, and in a quick maneuver, Richard Price was heading out to deep water of the Pacific Ocean.

54

About three hours from the marina, the roar of the boat engines quieted as Ryan slowly re-gained a bit of consciousness. Trying to focus his eyes and remember what had happened, everything seemed like a dream sequence until he heard Agent Tyler moan and he looked to his right. In the bunk across from him, Ryan through his blurry vision saw his companion Agent Tyler lying face down with her hands tied behind her back. As he lay on his back with his wrists tied together under him, Ryan twisted and pulled at his bindings trying to loosen them.

Feeling that time was not on his side, Ryan rolled off the bunk and placed his feet on the cabin floor trying to stand as the ocean swells rocked the boat violently. Trying to stand only to fall back on the bunk again, Ryan looked at the cabin doorway when he heard, "Hello Detective Ryan, a little groggy are we?"

"What now Price? We do a little fishing, or do you intend to throw us out in the middle of the ocean and watch us drown?"

"Nothing that simple Detective. If I did that they would continue to hunt for me and that would not fit into my final plan. I would much rather they think we all died together out here on the ocean, from a tragic un-foreseen accidental explosion caused by a gas leak on this old piece of shit boat. Or maybe they might think that I did go crazy and commit suicide taking you and Agent Tyler with me."

"And I suppose you and your crew will just swim off into the sunset never to be seen again?"

Laughing as he answered, Price said, "My crew will be burned beyond recognition floating right along with you and your companion there."

"Oh, did your crew know that was part of the deal signing on for this voyage? Did they know they had to give their lives for their loyal boss?"

"Actually, as I handed each one their bonus money for bringing you and your partner to me on a silver platter, we toasted with a very special drink. Unfortunately for them theirs contained a very deadly poison that made them dead to the world with no further need for their services."

"So, you're just going to light the fuse on this old tug and jump overboard and catch a ride on the first big fish that's heading towards safety?"

"Very funny Ryan, funny that you can joke at a time like this. You know Detective; I never cared much for those animals of the Prescott family, but one day when I was feeling all mushy inside, I promised Anthony that I would somehow even the score and make you pay for the lives of the Prescott's. I always keep my word. And besides, I've enjoyed this whole game of cat and mouse with the idea of the mouse roaring away and the cat meeting doom."

"How about that, the sick avenging the sick."

Again laughter filled the air and Price in a gesture held out both his hands and said, "Take a good look around Ryan, because this is the end of the line for you. All the years of being a good cop and this is what you get--- a date with the fishes."

"I may be just a stupid cop, but I see a flaw in your plan Price."

"And what might that be Detective?"

"If your body isn't found the authorities will continue to search for you assuming that you made your getaway."

"Ah, but they will find a body. Not mine, but one that fits my description to a tee."

"One of your crew I assume?"

`"Very good Ryan, that's why you get the big money for your job, good detective work."

"They'll find you Price. The forensic science that exists today will prove that it's not your body, and then they'll hunt you down and you will die just like that scum, the Prescott's."

For the first time in the conversation Price seemed annoyed by Ryan's arrogance.

"Did I get to you Price? Do you realize that you fucked up in your planning?"

"No Ryan, just thinking about the time. My ride should be here shortly and I don't want to keep him waiting."

As Ryan tried again to stand, he fell backwards onto the bunk again.

Price laughed again and said, "Let me help you Detective Ryan."

Walking toward the bunk Price removed a small hypodermic syringe from his pocket and injected Ryan right through his shirt sleeve and said, "This should take the edge off, but you'll be awake for the end."

Lying back down, Ryan felt the effect of whatever it was that he was injected with and could only focus his eyes on the ceiling above. Price had gone back up on deck to complete the preparation for his departure.

Tyler slowly opened her eyes and looked around at her surroundings and tried to get Ryan's attention.

Hearing her call his name in a low voice, Ryan turned his head, trying to focus on his companion, but the drug was strong and left him unable to respond.

As she twisted and pulled on her wrist restraints, Tyler noticed that her ankles were also tied together. Along with the waves splashing hard against the boat rocking it side to side, there was now yelling and loud conversation coming from up on deck. The shouting went on for several minutes and then it was followed by two gunshots. Expecting to see Price walk through the doorway of the cabin, Tyler was shocked to see the crewman Greg stumbled in with blood on the front of his shirt.

Greg said, "I think I killed the bastard, I threw him overboard after I hit him. He tried to poison Larry and me but I fooled him, I only sipped a little of that shit he gave me and spit it out. I don't drink any alcohol no more, but poor Larry he's dead. I don't know what that shit was but it knocked me out for a little while. He told me it was apple juice but he lied to us."

Tyler told Greg, "Untie tie us now."

"Lady, only if you promise that I won't be in trouble for what I did?"

"We will talk about that later. Now untie us."

"I ain't stupid lady. Now promise or you can blow up on this boat with your friend."

Tyler yelled out, "BLOW UP. What the hell are you talking about?"

"There's a bomb on this boat somewhere and it's going to blow up soon. Now promise or I'll leave you here and I'm going to get in the life raft and row away."

'Okay. What's your name?"

"Greg."

"Greg, I promise I will do everything I can to help you, and I will tell the police you saved our lives. Now untie us quickly so we can find that bomb."

After he unties Tyler, she then went to Ryan's aid and did the same for him. Ryan asked her, "Bonnie, take me up on deck please, I need some fresh air."

When they walked up on deck, what they saw was a gruesome and bloody mess. The body of Larry was laid out on the aft deck with both of his hands chopped off at the wrists.

Greg said, "The life raft is gone."

Tyler asked, "Are you sure you killed Price?"

Greg looked over the stern of the boat and said, "I think so, maybe not, maybe he got away in the life raft."

55

As Tyler helped Ryan to a chair up on deck, Greg looked for the hidden bomb. Tyler questioned Greg about the gun shots they had heard as she helped look for the bomb, but he just waved her off and said, "He fired at me twice but he only hit me once, it's not bad."

With Tyler's assistance the pair looked for a couple minutes and then strapped on life vests and decided it was time to abandon the boat before they were all blown up with the vessel. Just as they were about to lower themselves into the water, Greg told Tyler and Ryan, "Hey, I just remembered, there are two blow up life rafts in the bow of the boat."

Tyler said, "I saw a yellow raft all cut up lying on the galley floor but it's not good for anything."

Greg said, "Yeah but there's another one hidden in the anchor rope locker in the bow. I saw it yesterday when I was looking around."

As Ryan and Tyler waited to hear from Greg, and the thought of them all bobbing up and down in the ocean became a real possibility, they were so relieved to see him come out of the cabin with a big yellow bundle under his arm.

Ryan blurted out, "I hope that thing has its own air supply or we're fucked."

Greg undid the strap and pulled the safety pin and the raft began to fill with air. Tied in a small canvas bag was a fold-up oar that fell into the water as they lowered the raft off the back of the boat. It was quickly retrieved by Tyler who dove into the water after it.

Greg held the tie rope as Ryan climbed into the small raft, and then slowly lowered himself in, being careful not to capsize the rubber dingy. Tyler climbed up on the teak platform that was attached to the stern and then climbed into the raft.

Tyler was the first to row and she was very proficient at it, with smooth strokes that moved them away from the boat at a quick pace. At about fifty yards away, first there was a small explosion soon followed by a much larger explosion and a giant fireball that caused a wave that tipped the raft over, dumping all three passengers into the sea.

Debris from the explosion started showering down almost immediately, and a burning hull was all that remained of the sport fishing boat. Ryan and Greg helped Tyler into the raft after turning it right side up. By the time the other two pulled themselves into the rubber dingy, the hull and most of the boat's remains had sunk or drifted away, leaving nothing but the yellow raft and its passengers floating miles out to sea with no land in sight. To make matters worse, the oar had also floated away.

Paddling with nothing more then their hands they made their way to a few pieces of floating wood that appeared to be from a smashed cabin door. Pulling the door apart they were able to use the longer boards as oars.

With only the sun in the sky they determined which way to head, but the current was very strong and they weren't making any headway. After an hour of paddling it seemed hopeless. It wasn't until a large fishing boat called the Brandi Marlin came into view and was headed their way did they feel like they were saved.

Not known at the time to Ryan and company, they had been approximately thirty miles out to sea about five miles west of the closest island. The explosion had been seen by dozens of fishing boats in the area and a search for survivors had been in progress.

Once aboard the fishing boat Tyler identified herself to the captain of the Brandi Marlin as an FBI agent and Ryan as an LAPD detective. She requested the captain to contact the Coast Guard immediately and for them to start an immediate search for a man named Price who was also on a life raft. Explaining the importance of a quick response of the Coast Guard to try and apprehend Price, the captain radioed the Coast Guard and the local police in Avalon on Catalina Island.

By the time the Coast Guard cutter arrived on the scene, got all the information and made their way to Catalina Island, Price already abandoned his boat and was blending in with the tourists on the island.

After purchasing a ticket for the Catalina Ferry, Price casually walked around looking in shops and having a snack. Finding a public restroom on the outskirts of town, Price looked around to see if he was being observed by anyone. With his carry-on bag on his shoulder, Price made his way to a closed-in stall and started his transformation that was planned well in advance.

Entering the restroom as a dark haired slim middle aged man, Price exited as a much older gray haired man limping and using a cane to assist him walking back towards the pier just in time to board the ferry.

While on the Coast Guard cutter, Greg was taken into custody and when he was being searched for weapons it was discovered that he had been shot in the stomach by Price and lost a lot of blood.

Agent Tyler kept her word and when Greg was turned over to the captain of the boat she told him, "Take good care of him. The reason we're alive is because he saved our lives."

After contacting her supervisor, Agent Tyler turned her attention to Ryan and said, "Maybe after all this calms down and we lock that son of a bitch up, we can go on a real fishing trip."

Ryan said, "If it's all the same to you, I'd rather get my fish at the market and let the fish in the sea live a long life."

56

Two FBI Agents who flew in by helicopter had met the Coast Guard boat carrying Ryan, Tyler and Greg, at the dock and the trio was quickly taken to a secure location for questioning. The Harbor Patrol and several island police were also waiting for the story on the explosion, but everything was hush, hush until a decision was made on which way to handle matters.

After the explanation by Agent Tyler, the orders to search Catalina Island were issued and all out going boats searched. Several hours went by and the out cry of the people wanting to get back to the mainland won out and boats were once again able to leave.

A security camera at the ticket sales counter had recorded Price purchasing a ticket but by the time it was discovered, Price had already made his way back to the mainland and then to Marina del Rey. Once the Catalina Ferry had docked Price hooked up with a boat owner he had hired to meet him and paid the man handsomely to take him up the coast to the marina.

Because of Price's connection to Marina del Rey, a thorough search of the marina was put into action. As pictures of Richard Price were being circulated around the marina, no one paid any attention to the medium sized sailboat slowly making its way out to sea.

Price had hired two experienced deckhands for his voyage, and was enjoying a cocktail on the deck of his sailing vessel as he monitored police calls on his newly acquired special band radio.

As the days went on, reports of Price sightings came in from Catalina and Marina del Rey, but the most important call came from a man named Eldred Wisco three days later. Mr. Wisco reported that he had rented his sailboat to a man named Taylor, who fit the description and looked very much like the circulated picture posted around the marina.

Finding the slip empty the FBI notified the Coast Guard to orchestrate a search for the missing sailboat that had left the marina earlier in the week.

Unfortunately for all involved the sailboat in question was long gone and thoughts of capturing Richard Price were gone with it.

The FBI, US Coast Guard, Interpol, and the LAPD bloodhound Detective Bob Ryan were dumbfounded.

It had been three months that passed by and Richard Price had appeared to have dropped off the face of the earth with no contact from him at all and no more sightings anywhere. The owner of the sailboat Price rented had offered a reward for information leading to its return.

A story had appeared in an Acapulco newspaper of a boat fitting the description being used by pirates off the coast of Guatemala. By the time the authorities had a chance to check the reports out the vessel had disappeared once again. Price was into the wind and from all appearances he was not going to return to the United States, but one man knew he would be back, but just not when.

57

While preparing for a long weekend getaway to Las Vegas with Agent Tyler, Ryan looked in the mirror and noticed that his mustache and what was left of his once full head of hair needed a slight touch up. The gray of his hair was something normal for a man of sixty-five, but to Ryan it was unacceptable.

After a quick application of a popular hair-coloring product and a quick shower he packed up his necessary grooming aides and his medications. His meds consisted of aspirin and Lipitor for his high cholesterol, vitamins for his energy, and Viagra for his stamina.

The reservations were made at the MGM Grand, which included very expensive front row seats to the stage show that was the number one attraction in town that weekend. A romantic couple of days together forgetting about police or bureau business were something they both were looking forward to. They couldn't wait to get on the airplane.

Ryan and Tyler had gone out many times for dinner or a movie over the past three months, and it appeared that things between them were getting very serious. A quick phone call from Ryan to Tyler to confirm that she was on her way to meet him at Burbank Airport proved to be a total disaster. After a somewhat cool response, Tyler said, "He's back. The son of a bitch is back."

"Price? Price is back?"

"While checking video tapes from the border at San Ysidro, an alert border guard spotted our man Price walking through the border check point and called it in."

"Are they positive it was him?"

"Get this. He looked straight at the camera and gave it a one finger salute and smiled."

"They are checking further Tyler to see if he's spotted getting into a vehicle?"

"One of our field agents, Paul Krause out of San Diego, is following up on the sighting and so far all they know is he appeared to be alone."

"Guess that means *our* getaway is down the crapper for now?"

"It's okay Ryan, we'll get there someday. How about we meet for breakfast at Denny's? I can be at the one on Sepulveda Blvd. in a half hour.

After meeting in the Denny's parking lot, Agent Tyler and Ryan were walking to the entrance when she got another call from her office, "Hold on Ryan while I find out what this is about."

A couple minutes went by when she said, "We got something more on Price."

"Please tell me you know where he's at?"

"Not quite, but one of the security cameras on the far side of the border crossing showed him getting into a pick-up truck and the lab is working on an ID by enhancing the license plate."

"Oh crap. How long has it been since he crossed the border?"

"Approximately thirty-seven hours."

"He could be anywhere by now."

"Ryan, I've been ordered to report in at the office. I'll call you later if there are any new developments."

"Okay, I guess I'd better check in also and find out if the LAPD has anything new, right after I get something to eat. Are you sure you don't want to get a quick bite before you go?"

With a kiss on his cheek she said, "I got to go, see you later."

Ryan said, "Okay, I'll call you later sweetheart."

58

Lake Balboa is a fairly new recreational facility located in the San Fernando Valley, which is located just a little north and over the mountain from downtown Los Angeles, California.

The concrete lake bed which was constructed in the Sepulveda Basin is filled with reclaimed water that flows from the wash to the north. The water is run through a filtration plant making it safe for the environment and is then stocked with several varieties of fish. It is also the home and nesting place for many types of fowl. Every weekend of every month you can find fishermen of all ages and picnickers surrounding the lake. Enjoying the many ideal locations for just relaxing has become a blessing to the habitants of the valley.

As the Sun was coming up on an expected beautiful Saturday morning, the Park Ranger noticed something very peculiar. The melody of the early rising chirping birds was nonexistent and the sound around the lake was dead silent.

Driving his service truck down by the lake's edge he could not believe his eyes. It appeared that every living thing on or around the lake was dead. Thousands of fish and birds of all types were floating on the still water. Dead birds littered the path and the grassy knolls at the lake's edge.

With panic in his voice he first called his immediate supervisor who in turn called the local police. The initial investigation revealed that all the fish and fowl had been poisoned, but further tests would be taken to determine how and who carried it out.

As the morning progressed, the calls started pouring into 911 reporting the incident. The most important of all the calls was the one claiming responsibility for the deed.

Richard Price was back in town and he wanted every living soul to know it and that he held their very lives in his hands.

59

As Ryan sat at an early morning briefing at the PAB, his cell phone started buzzing away with no caller ID available.

Ignoring the call Ryan replaced his cell in his inside jacket pocket. A couple minutes went by when it started buzzing away again. Once more Ryan just ignored it and placed it back in his pocket.

With the Police Commissioner and the Chief of Police paying very close attention to a preliminary report by the representative from the Poison Control Center, Ryan listened carefully about the unknown poison used at the Sepulveda Basin.

It had only been five minutes since Ryan's last unanswered phone call on his cell phone, and as he sat taking notes, he noticed the Watch Commander come in and whisper something to the Chief.

After a few words with the Commissioner, the Chief asked Ryan to join him and the Commissioner in the next room excusing him from the briefing.

Closing the door behind him Ryan asked, "What's this all about Chief?"

"Detective Ryan, when your phone buzzes again, answer it please."

As Ryan started once again to ask, his phone began to buzz. Looking at the caller ID, he said, "Ryan here, who's this?"

"Hello Detective Ryan, my old friend."

"Price, what do you want, you psychopath?"

"Now, now Detective, no name calling, at least not for now. After you hear what I have to say, you may actually think very highly of me."

"Price, the only way I'll think highly of you is when I hear that your rotting corpse was found floating in the bay."

Followed by laughter, Price said, "Did you like my little water trick this morning?"

"I knew you had something to do with that."

The Chief asked Ryan, "Can you put him on speaker phone?"

"Sorry Chief. This old cell phone of mine isn't equipped with one."

The Chief said, "Let me speak to him."

Ryan handed his phone to the Chief and smiled slightly as he sat back in his chair.

"This is Chief Walton. Who am I talking with?"

"Well hello Chief, this is Richard Price and how are you this morning?"

"Price, what the hell is this all about?"

"I just wanted to get your attention Chief. Was I successful?"

"Turn yourself in Price, stop this madness and save your life."

Followed by laughter, Price said, "Save my life? I want to save your life, and every other life in this city."

"What are you talking about?"

"My little showing of how powerful my toxins are was just a small sample of what would happen if I poisoned the city reservoirs."

Not knowing how to respond to that statement the chief calmly asked, "What is it that you want Price? How do we put an end to all this senseless killing?"

"Did that get to you chief? Do I have your full attention now?"

"You have my full attention Price, but what is it that you actually want?"

Followed by more laughter, Price just said, "I'll call again after you've had time to digest what I hold in my power. When I call again we will make arrangements for a conference call so I can talk with the decision makers of the city. Now please hand the phone back to Detective Ryan."

Taking the phone from the Chief, Ryan asked, "What do you want Price?"

"Just to be friends, detective, at least for the time being. After our short friendship and meeting on the boat I was depressed to see the way it ended. I'll want you and that bitch you're hanging around with these days to join me again, it's that simple. I'm going to kill you both. Since our boating trip was such a failure we need to try again. Like they say if at first you don't succeed."

Ryan lost it and said, "Fuck you Price."

"Now there you go again losing your temper. You have a nice day detective."

The call ended and Ryan threw his cell phone across the room at the wall, watching it burst into many pieces. Looking at the chief he said, "The next phone will have all the modern shit, chief."

Chief Walton said, "That was uncalled for, Det. Ryan. We are supposed to be professionals here and not stoop to those levels. This man obviously has a vendetta against you and Agent Tyler. I will personally call the FBI and fill them in. You, Ryan, *will* purchase a new phone and report any communication you have with Price. Now, unless you have something else to say, this meeting is over."

60

Three days went by before Richard Price contacted Ryan again but this time the detective was equipped with a new cell phone. The new piece of equipment was state of the art and was monitored by a tracking device supplied by the FBI.

"Hello Detective Ryan, how are we doing this morning?"

"I'm doing fine Price, and you are one day closer to rotting in prison waiting for the pellet to drop in the gas chamber, or if you're lucky, a quick needle in the arm."

"Wow! Did you get up on the wrong side of Agent Tyler? How is that sweet princess, is she taking care of all your needs?"

"What do you want you bastard, I'm busy trying to track down real criminals, not scum like you? Call the FBI. They're the ones that want to talk with you. Call me when you're ready to turn yourself in. I'm busy, good bye."

Hanging up on Price was something Ryan knew would infuriate him but would push him to call back and hopefully would keep him on the line even longer than the first call. Within one minute Ryan's phone started buzzing away with a caller ID that said unknown.

When he answered Ryan said, "Yeah what can I do for you?"

"Do not hang up on me again detective. You won't like the consequences."

"Hold on Price, I'll be right with you."

Yelling out over his shoulder to an empty desk, Ryan said, "Make my ham sandwich on rye with Swiss and mustard. Oh yeah, some potato salad and a pickle, a well cooked one from the bottom of the barrel."

Speaking back into the phone Ryan asked, "Can I get you something Price? You know something to kill your dumb ass."

"Don't play games with me detective. I know what you're trying to do."

"Yeah I'm trying to get you lunch Price. Meet me in my office and we'll talk over old times."

Studying the read-out on his cell, Ryan pinned down the location where Price's call was coming from. According to the address on the phone readout, he was located in a run down commercial area of Sun Valley that Ryan was familiar with. The area only had deserted buildings and vacant lots with most of the properties fenced in.

Ryan had to ask, "Okay Price. What is it that you really want?"

"I want a meeting detective. Just you and me."

"Are you crazy? Oh wait a minute. I forgot. You are crazy."

"If you want to save a lot of lives detective, you'll stop playing games with me. You and I will meet at a place I choose or I will kill more people to get your attention."

"Why me Price?

"Have you forgotten my brother's in-laws? I haven't. You were responsible for the death of the poor Prescott clan, and I promised my brother I would make you pay."

"You are crazy Price, and so were the Prescott's. It must be in the genes and you have just enough to turn you into a real nut case."

Suddenly realizing how long he had been on the phone with Ryan, Price quickly said, "I'll call you back tomorrow" and then ended the call.

Ryan called the FBI office and talked to Tyler and asked, "Did you get it sweetheart?"

"Yeah Ryan, I got it. What the hell was the hanging up on him all about? You could have lost him with that stunt."

"Yeah, yeah, did you get the location? I'm very familiar with that place. It's a bad area of Sun Valley."

"There are a couple of undercover cars on the way to that end of the valley as we speak."

"Good, but you know he'll be gone by the time they get there?"

"We have something else to talk about Ryan. Meet me at Art's Deli in Studio City and I'll fill you in on the progress we've made on the poison the asshole is using."

"How about I meet you there in one hour?"

"That sounds good. I should have some info on the Sun Valley location by then. Wear your best tie Ryan."

Ryan laughed, "Just a tie sweetheart? Don't yah think I'll draw too much attention to my, let's say family jewels?"

"Not a big distraction Ryan. You worry too much about the little things."

Still laughing, "Very funny you sweet bundle of joy. See you there in an hour."

256

61

Art's Deli is a favorite eatery in the San Fernando Valley. Frequented by many in the movie industry, its location on Ventura Blvd. in Studio City is not far from Beverly Hills, or the true homes of so many actors who live in the hills of Studio City and Sherman Oaks.

By the time Tyler arrived at Art's, Ryan was already seated in a booth in the rear with a view of the entrance. As she approached the booth Ryan stood up and said, "You made good time. You're only a half hour late."

Responding with a smile she said, "Thanks wiseass. The traffic coming into this valley sucks; I had to crawl along like a snail because of one stinking accident that took out about ten vehicles.

All traffic was forced to exit onto Sepulveda Blvd., which was like a parking lot and then for some reason the Ventura Freeway was backed up, I hate driving into the valley."

With their brief conversation interrupted by the waitress, who asked, "Are you now ready to order?" Ryan responded with, "Just give us one minute please."

Tyler asked without looking at the menu, "What do you recommend Ryan?"

"Corned beef on rye with a cup of chicken noodle soup on the side is my favorite. But to each his own, I've heard everything in this place is good. Their rice pudding hits the spot too."

Making it simple for the waitress, Tyler ordered the same as Ryan with the exception of a cup of coffee instead of Ryan's Egg Cream selection.

Folding his hands in front of him on the table, Ryan finally asked. "Okay, what's the news you have for me on Price, please tell me he's dead. It will help the food go down?"

"Price was gone by the time our agents got to Sun Valley, no surprise. What they did find however was some homeless guy who remembered Price getting into a white or light colored van and driving away. No make or license number but it was something."

"So he got away again huh? Do you want to spoil my appetite?"

"I do have something that may help your appetite Hon."

"Please tell me he died in a flaming crash with a semi and then we can toast the occasion."

"Not quite. The lab found the antidote that completely nullifies the poison he's been threatening us with."

"Well now you got my attention, it's not as good as his death, but at least it will save other lives. That is what you're telling me, right?"

"It was right in our possession all the time."

"What do you mean?"

"Several of Price's accomplices had aspirin bottles or packets in their possession when they were apprehended or killed. The phony aspirin was actually something called True Blue #1436. We knew of its existence from documents obtained from Price's pharmaceutical files but we couldn't find anything in the labs of the three pharmaceutical buildings owned by Price."

"Aspirins? We're going to need a shit load of aspirins to dilute hundreds of gallons that madman is threatening to use in the reservoirs of Los Angeles."

"It's not real aspirins Ryan, this stuff was packaged to look like aspirins including a familiar marking on the pills themselves and the yellow labels on the bottles and packets. Our investigators located what they believe to be some of his main stock pile of the poison. They also found cases of the antidote one mile from the manufacturing pharmaceutical facility in Louisiana."

Ryan asked, "Only some of the poison?"

"They found two fifty-five gallon drums of the shit, but according to Price he had more than twice that."

"What about the warehouse in Sun Valley where he called from, was there anything there to help us?"

"Nothing. Looks like he just happened to pick that spot to call from, but we'll keep it under surveillance for a while. From the looks of the place the agents said he must have been living there for a while."

"Well, it looks like all we have to do now is find the bastard."

As their food was placed on the table, Ryan said, "Bon appetite my dear."

Ryan and Agent Tyler spent the rest of the day together visiting the poison control center and the federal building in West Los Angeles. With no contact from Richard Price, and no additional information learned from the Sun Valley location, all they could do was wait and hope that no more innocent people would die at the hands of the crazed killer.

62

Holding true to his ways, Richard Price had not made contact with Ryan or anyone else in the police department or the FBI in over two weeks. Working a double homicide with his new partner at the LAPD, Sgt. Peter Stevens, Ryan was actually glad not to hear from Price and hoped that the FBI had taken over his capture completely.

The crime scene of the recent homicide was located in an office loft on Ventura Blvd. in Sherman Oaks. The vacant shop below was a one-time highly successful aerobics gym, but due to high rent and lack of customers with big bucks to spend, the business failed and had to close its doors permanently.

The two victims were bound and gagged in a kitchen area tied securely to high back chairs. Each had been shot execution style with one bullet to the back of the head. With no signs of forced entry, it was assumed that the victims knew their killer or killers.

While Ryan and his new partner questioned potential witnesses from the surrounding buildings, the crime scene investigators meticulously did their job. The only lead came from a transient who had been sleeping in front of the doorway of the vacant store. Although it took many questions and a few bucks to grease the palm of the fulltime bum, Ryan got a possible ID on the shooter's vehicle.

The old wino by chance was a one-time auto mechanic and was familiar with old cars. It was easy for him to recognize the 1965 Chevy Impala, but couldn't remember if it was black, dark blue, or any other dark color. When asked if the driver was alone in the car or if there was another person, the old guy said, "Actually, there was a pretty young girl driving and she smiled at me earlier when I asked her for some change."

"You mean you talked to her?" Ryan asked."

"Yeah, and she told me to fuck-off. So I went to lie down on my blanket and catch some Z's."

"Okay Pops. You think you could describe to me what they looked like?"

"You get me a little taste, and I will. You'd be surprised at how much better my memory is when I jolt those brain cells with a little taste, detective."

"How about if we lock you up in a nice warm cell for a few days. You know, just until the shakes get real bad, and then we turn you loose to go and find your own taste?"

The old guy scratched his head and said, "No, I wouldn't like that. I just want to go and mind my own business if that's okay with you?"

"There's always another plan Pops. That's the one where you give me and my partner a real good detailed description of the man and woman you saw in that car. Then you go on your way with a nice crisp twenty in your pocket."

"I like that way better detective. I think I'm starting to remember real good now."

Ryan called his partner over and introduced him to his new-found friend.

"Sgt. Stevens, this is Pops. Pops, this is Sgt. Stevens. The Sergeant here is going to take down your description of the people you saw in that old Chevy. When you're done, you sit your ass down on your blanket and I'll see you before we take off. You got that Pops?"

"You won't forget what you promised me, right detective?"

"I won't forget Pops. Now don't you leave anything out that we talked about?"

Ryan told his partner, "Pete, I'm going upstairs to see how the crime scene guys are doing. Get his story down on paper and get some ID on him also. We may need him later for a positive ID on the suspects if we catch up to them."

"Ryan. Shouldn't we take him to the house and get a complete statement from him on tape?"

"You want to put his funky ass in your car for the trip to the station house? You won't get the smell out with ten of those Christmas trees hanging on your mirror."

"Gotcha boss. Hey Pops. What yah got for me?"

63

It had been fourteen hours since Ryan started his workday at 7AM that morning and with the new homicide dumped in his lap, there was just so much that the old brain could compute without rest. After calling Agent Tyler and finding out she would be working through the night, he was done for the day.

Heading back home to Woodland Hills, Ryan stopped at a Subway Sub Shop to pick up a sandwich, chips and a drink for his nighttime snack before turning in.

The traffic to the West Valley was light, so the drive back home was a pleasant one for the overly tired detective.

Pulling in to his driveway he noticed that all the lights were out in the main house. It was nothing unusual for that late at night, but it was strange that the porch light was also out.

Around back Ryan noticed that the light was on in the kitchen and it appeared that Dorothy was still up from the movement noticed through the side window.

Ryan whistled for Brandy, but there was no response from his loyal companion. Every night, no matter what the time was, Brandy would run to Ryan's car when he pulled in the driveway.

Cautiously walking up the steps of the rear porch, Ryan opened the screen door and knocked on the glass window pane calling out, "Dot it's me, everything okay?"

Opening the unlocked door Ryan was greeted by Brandy jumping up and Dorothy saying. "Oh darn! I forgot to open the doggie door after the man from the gas company came this afternoon."

"You also forgot to turn on the front porch light Dot."

"No, I know I turned it on Robert. The bulb must have blown out."

"Where do you keep the bulbs?"

"In the Pantry next to the stove dear."

"I'll change it for you and then Brandy and I are going to split a sandwich and turn in for the night."

"Oh Robert. The man from the gas company had to go in your apartment but I stayed there with him while he checked out your stove and fireplace."

"What reason did he give for wanting to check things out Dot?"

"I had called the gas company to send someone out dear, just to make sure everything was working properly. You know its been a long time since the gas had been turned on up there."

"How long ago did you call Dot, I've been living here six months already. I thought they did an inspection a couple of weeks after I first moved in?"

"I kind of remember that too. But when I mentioned that to the man, he said it was a follow-up and it was just a routine visit."

"Do me a favor Dot and keep Brandy here with you until I check my place out and make sure all is safe."

"Robert you don't think…"

"Just to be safe Dot. Please give the gas company a call and see if they sent out a man to check things out. I know it may sound foolish, but with all the things that have happened since my return, let's play it safe."

"I'll be right back Dot."

Walking up the steps to his apartment, Ryan took out his service weapon just to be prepared in case his suspicions were correct that he was walking into a trap. Gently trying to turn the doorknob, Ryan found it locked and he had to use his key.

Entering the house slowly with his weapon still in his right hand, he walked to the table by the couch and turned on the light. Visually checking out the main room first, he then entered the bedroom and turned on the light switch just inside the doorway.

All appeared normal just the way he left it that morning. His bed was unmade, pajama bottoms and t-shirt lying side by side next to the blanket. Next he checked out the bathroom and it too looked normal.

Holstering his weapon, Ryan realized he was being a little over cautious and headed for the door to go and retrieve Brandy and his sandwich he had left in Dot's kitchen.

Ryan was about to reenter the rear porch screen door when the explosion behind him from his apartment knocked him off the steps to the ground and flaming debris was falling all around him.

The garage apartment and the tree next to the steps were engulfed in flames and pieces of glass and wood had splintered the rear of the house. Some of the splinters struck Ryan in the back, ass and neck. With the sharp pains he was feeling he knew he had to move quickly and get help. He crawled back up the steps onto the back porch floor of the house.

As Dorothy opened the door she asked, "What happened Robert?" Ryan yelled to her, "Call 911, quickly Dot."

"Robert you're bleeding, you need help."

"Call 911 now, hurry. Tell them there is also an officer down besides the fire."

Ryan was silent after that, passing out with Brandy at his side licking his face.

64

The murmured sounds appearing to come from a distant place were the first thing Ryan heard before he opened his eyes. His blurred vision along with the almost total darkness surrounding him did not make it easy to focus on where he was.

It took several minutes of trying to adjust to the small bit of light coming from a door that was partially open. Putting things together, Ryan determined he was in a hospital bed.

Trying to call out he found that it was impossible because of a small tube that had been inserted in his mouth taped in place providing him with oxygen.

As he lifted his right arm to remove the tube from his mouth, Ryan noticed there was a needle taped to his hand with another tube attached to an IV bag hanging on a stand next to the bed. Looking to his side he saw and heard a monitor that was giving off beeps and he realized he had additional wires and tubes connected to his chest. Reaching down between his legs he felt the tube that was inserted in his penis and thought to him self, not again.

Feeling around the side railings in the dark, he found the control for the light, TV, bed and call for the nurse button. In less than a minute a nurse appeared, turned on the light and said, "How are we doing Mr. Ryan?"

Pointing at the tube in his mouth Ryan made gestures to the nurse to remove it. When she shook her head no, he removed it himself peeling the tape away that held it in place.

As the nurse first pushed the button for assistance and then tried to reinstall the oxygen tube, Ryan found the strength to yell out, "GET THE HELL AWAY FROM ME I DON'T NEED THE GODDAMN THING."

It took only a few minutes for the doctor on call to make his way to the room. "What's happening here nurse?" he asked.

"Mr. Ryan has decided he doesn't need oxygen doctor, so he removed the tube himself."

"This won't work Mr. Ryan. You need the oxygen tube reinstalled."

Ryan with a gravelly voice said, "Try it Doc and I pull it out and shove it up your ass. Now where the hell am I and how long have I been here?"

"Okay Mr. Ryan, have it your way."

"First of all Doc. It's Detective Ryan. And second, who the hell are you?"

"Sorry Detective. I'm Dr. Richards. You were brought into Emergency two nights ago, unconscious with massive bleeding on the back of your head, neck and backside that required immediate surgery."

Reaching around with his left hand Ryan touched the back of his head and felt the bandages for the first time.

The Doctor continued. "From what I've heard, there was an explosion at your home and you were knocked unconscious."

"Was anyone else injured Doc?"

"I don't have any other information detective, but I'll check."

"Thanks Doc. I need to call my Captain and let him know that I'm back among the living."

"I'll make sure he's contacted, detective. Now what I need from you is a little cooperation."

"No tube Doc."

"No tube. But we're going to try an oxygen mask for a little while until you're a little more stable because your levels on the machine aren't stable enough yet."

"Okay Doc. I can use a little TV time anyway. It helps me sleep."

After dozing off for what seemed like only a few minutes, Ryan awoke with the feel of someone gently rubbing his left hand. Turning his head slightly to the left and focusing his eyes he saw Dorothy Metzger and Tyler standing by the bed.

Smiling a little Ryan asked, "How's the room service in this place Ladies?"

As the tears rolled down Dorothy's cheeks, Tyler removed her hand from Ryan's and said, "And I thought you were really hurt this time."

"I'm fine sweetheart, just a little hole in the back of my head."

Smiling back at him Tyler responded, "Now you have a matching pair."

Ryan asked, "How is the house Dot?"

"I've already fixed up your room in the house. Your apartment and the garage are completely gone. The fire department and ambulance arrived shortly after you passed out, Robert. Everything will be fine. Don't you worry about it."

"I have some money saved Dot. It will come in handy to rebuild everything."

"Robert forget it. Your room is in the house from now on where I can keep an eye on you."

"We'll talk, Dot, after I get out of this place. By the way, have either one of you seen that doctor who was here a few minutes before you came?"

"Robert, I've been here for two hours and Bonnie got here an hour ago. I talked to the Doctor when I got here and haven't seen him since."

"Wow Dot, I must have slept a little longer than I thought. Did he happen to mention how much longer I would be enjoying his hospitality in this establishment?"

Tyler chuckled a little and said, "You're here for at least a week sweetheart, so lie back and enjoy it. When you get out you and I have some unfinished business with a Mr. Price."

"You got a lead on him Hun? You know where he's hiding?"

"Sure do Ryan. His ass is sitting in a holding cell in a Federal Building that doesn't even exist on the books."

Looking at Dorothy, Tyler said, "You never heard that Mrs. Metzger."

"Please call me Dot and you forget, I was married to one of you people with a badge for many years. Is this Price the one responsible for all the trouble Robert's been getting into?"

Ryan said, "One and the same Dot. That madman is responsible for killing hundreds of innocent people."

"Good. I hope you fry the bastard."

"That will still be up to a Judge and Jury, but I think it will be a done deal."

Ryan smiled a little and said, "I'm sorry ladies, but I think one of these tubes is carrying some kind of shit that wants me to sleep and I just feel like closing my eyes. Maybe we can talk more later?"

Both women kissed Ryan on the cheek and told him they would visit him the next day. With no argument, Ryan closed his eyes and said, "Sounds good, see you tomorrow."

As Dot and Bonnie left the room they saw Chief Walton walking their way. Bonnie said, "He's doing fine Chief, but if you want to talk with him it will have to wait, his medication just kicked in and he's in la, la land now."

65

Ryan's hospital stay was a total of six days and he was chomping at the bit to get away from all the poking and prodding of the doctors and nurses. Tyler was the one who got the job of picking him up and bringing him back home to Woodland Hills.

When Tyler pulled into the driveway of the house, Ryan's response to seeing the burned down building where he once lived was, "Holy shit."

"Ryan, you have no idea how lucky you were."

"Hey, accidents happen Hon."

"This was no accident. I thought you knew that."

"Look Hon, all I've heard so far was that it was a gas leak. What else did you find?"

"The lab boys determined yesterday that it was a gas leak that blew your place to shit, but it was triggered by you when you opened the door with a five minute delay they guessed."

"Guessed?"

"There was not much to go by, so yeah, it was a guess considering the information they did have."

"Price huh?' Ryan asked.

"Price yes. Or one of his people."

"When do I get to see Mr. Price?"

"Give it a couple of days, okay sweetheart, until you're feeling stronger. He ain't going anywhere."

"What have your people got from him so far?"

"Nothing Ryan, absolutely nothing. He refuses to talk. He hasn't even asked for a lawyer."

"Well what the hell are you bringing me here for? Let's go see Mr. Price."

"Give it a couple more days Ryan, he's just starting to ripen a little, then he'll be right for the picking."

Still sitting in the car, Ryan asked, "What about the rest of his stock pile of poison that he was sitting on?"

"We don't know its where-a bouts yet, but I'm sure he'll use that as a bargaining tool. We're ready for his bullshit."

Ryan leaned over and kissed Tyler and asked, "Are you going to come up and tuck me into bed?"

Tyler smiled and said, "I've got better plans for you and your bed. My overnight bag is in the trunk Hon."

"Are you sure my body is ready for the abuse you're going to give it?"

"Abuse, I'll give you abuse, get the hell up stairs and get into that bed. I got a weeks vacation to work on you and hopefully get something in return."

"Oh, I have to reciprocate?"

"You're damn right Ryan, multiple orgasms every night and then breakfast in bed each morning."

"That's it! Take me back to the hospital."

Getting out of the car, Tyler walked to the trunk, opened it and took out her overnight bag and threw it at Ryan saying, "You carry the luggage sweetheart."

Dorothy was standing on the front porch watching the pair of senior law enforcement representatives acting like teenagers.

Walking hand in hand Ryan and Tyler quickly climbed the porch steps, looked at Dorothy and said in unison, "Hi Dot is our room ready?"

Laughing at their question Dorothy said, "Top of the stairs, end of the hallway breakfast at 7AM."

In the forty-eight hours that followed Ryan and Tyler found out much about each other, likes and dislikes, world politics, religious beliefs, and sexual desires. Their two uninterrupted days had been like a honeymoon without the wedding and was long overdue.

Each morning the two lovers would wake up to the smell of bacon cooking and coffee brewing in the kitchen. Dorothy would call to them from the bottom of the stairs that breakfast was being served in the dining room.

On the third morning all was quiet with no fragrant aromas drifting to the room above and no pleasant voice beckoning to come to the table.

Putting on his robe and walking down the stairs whistling the tune As Time Goes By from the movie Casablanca, Ryan entered the kitchen to find it empty. Walking out onto the back porch he looked out into the yard and saw nothing that appeared strange, until he spotted Brandy lying next to the apple tree in the far left corner of the yard.

Calling her name and whistling didn't get any response so he walked down the back steps to where she was curled up and motionless. Calling her name, "Brandy, come on girl," again got no movement from his trusted friend.

Bending down to check her Ryan noticed where the dog had thrown up a white and murky substance and when he lifted her head he realized that the dog was dead. Assuming that the dog had eaten something that contained poison, Ryan stood up slowly looking around the yard but saw nothing that appeared out of place or unusual.

Returning to the house Ryan was met by Tyler in the kitchen who asked when she saw the look on his face, "What's happened Hun?"

"Dot's not around and I just found Brandy dead in the backyard and I don't like the looks of this."

"Have you looked around yet for a note from Dot?"

"No I haven't but I think we need to get dressed and then try to figure this out."

Climbing the stairs to the second floor Ryan knocked on Dot's bedroom door several times before opening it and walking in. The bed was unmade and the French doors that led to the deck above the rear porch were wide open. Walking onto the deck Ryan looked to his left and saw the top of a ladder extending up over the edge of the railing.

Walking back to his bedroom Ryan found Tyler on her cell phone calling in a report to her office. Picking up his cell phone from the nightstand Ryan first called 911 for an instant response then called the West Valley police station. While getting dressed Ryan's cell phone started buzzing away. Looking at the caller ID it read, "Unknown." In an uncharacteristic way Ryan answered, "Yeah, who is it?"

"Well good morning detective, a little cranky this morning? Get up on the wrong side of Agent Tyler perhaps?"

Shocked at who was calling, Ryan said, "How did you get to use a phone Price?"

Stopping and just staring, Tyler who was still on the line with her office said into her phone, "I want an immediate check on Richard Price."

After a short response from whoever she was talking with Tyler said, "You heard me correctly, Price, Richard Price, we have him in custody or did he somehow escape?"

Switching his phone to speakerphone Ryan asked, "How the hell did you get out Price?"

Laughter was followed by heavy coughing, "I was never in detective, you have the wrong man in custody," followed by more laughter and coughing.

Ryan asked, "Where is Dorothy Metzger?"

More laughter followed by, "Your landlady is very near-by and she is still sleeping soundly. You and Agent Tyler were sleeping so nicely when my friends and I paid a visit early this morning so we didn't disturb you. I'm sorry about that mongrel dog of yours but I couldn't have her bark and spoil my surprise."

Tyler waved to get Ryan's attention. As Ryan covered his phone mouth piece she told him, "Price is still in the lock-up and he has no phone, I don't know what's going on but that can't be Price on the phone."

Removing his hand from the mouth piece and putting it back up to his ear he heard Price laughing again and uncontrollable coughing.

Ryan asked, "I don't know how you're doing this Price, but I think it's time you get to the point."

"My point detective, (cough, cough) is that I still want you dead, with as much suffering as possible. And for your question of how I'm doing it you need to check out the man that is being held in custody. I'm very surprised at you detective for not checking out the identity of the man they locked up. Didn't he tell you who he was? Oh I forgot, he's a mute, ha, ha, ha, (cough, cough) a cute mute at that, he looks just like me but I'm much smarter."

Ryan said to Tyler, "He says you have the wrong man in custody, he's a look-alike and he's a mute."

Tyler said, "Impossible."

Price said laughing, "Not so impossible. Ask Agent Tyler what they got when they ran his prints. I'll bet those prints didn't show up anywhere. Why you ask, because I'll tell you, the man has no record in this country. I have no record in this country. Isn't that funny? (cough, cough)"

"Price, why did you kidnap Mrs. Metzger? She's an innocent party in all of this. It's me you want Price, not her. Exchange her for me."

"In time detective, but for now I'll tell you this. I needed those few days you morons thought you had me in custody so you would drop your defenses and I could set up my plan. In that time I was able to visit three of the reservoirs around LA County and position a drum of my magic solution in place. Each drum is equipped with an explosive device that I can activate at anytime I choose."

Ryan yelled into his phone, "What the hell is it that you want Price?"

"I told you detective, I want you dead."

"But why Price, why go through all of this, killing so many innocent people. If it's me you want, take me, but give up this ridiculous quest of yours."

"You're talking into the wind Ryan your words are falling on deaf ears. (cough, cough)"

"Even you can't be that sick Price. What is it besides me that you want? It can't be money or recognition. You have all of that you need, so what else is it? I noticed you're doing a lot of coughing Price, could it be you're killing yourself with your own poison?"

"What I want Ryan, I have said many times, I want you dead before I die, before I take my last breath I want to see you suffer the way you have made other people suffer. My coughing is merely a little cold I contracted, nothing more."

Getting excited as he spoke Price started coughing and had a hard time regaining his composure, so Ryan tried to push his buttons a little more. "What would your mother have said for you acting this way Price? How about your father, would he have condoned your actions?"

Price continued coughing as he tried to get the words out but could only say, "You'll pay Ryan, cough, cough, you'll pay for those, cough, cough, remarks," as the call ended.

All the time Ryan was on the phone Tyler was trying to get a fix on Price's location but the phone he had been using was a throw-away and was probably just that, thrown away. Ryan said, "Your people need to get on whoever it is they have in custody and try and get something out of him, I don't think we have much time."

66

As Ryan and Tyler finished getting dressed the front doorbell was ringing and the street in front of the house was flooded with flashing lights. Within one hour there were investigators swarming through the house and over every inch of the property. A phone tap was set up on the house phone and on Ryan's cell phone.

The man being held by the FBI was once again interrogated, this time with someone in the room who could use sign language. After it was explained that Richard Price had already contacted the authorities the man opened up and revealed his deal with Price. He first revealed that he was to be paid a very large sum of money but would say no more. After being threatened with a long jail term he agreed to open up. Because what he did was still a crime the man would still be held in the federal lock-up

Ryan and Tyler watched the interrogation through a two way mirror and were both surprised at the uncanny resemblance the man had to Price. The promise that had been made by Price to the imposter was a deposit made in his name at an Acapulco bank in his native land in Mexico of one hundred thousand dollars.

In the two hours that had passed since Price's last call Ryan was a nervous wreck worrying about the safety of Dorothy Metzger. The investigations at the house had revealed nothing as to her whereabouts.

Upon leaving the Federal Building Ryan checked his cell phone for messages and found two. Complaining to Tyler about why cell phone reception in the Federal Building was blocked got only one response, "I don't make the rules sweetheart, but from what I've heard that will be changing soon."

All three messages were from, "Unknown," which Ryan knew had to be Price. Within ten minutes of Ryan and Tyler leaving the federal property Ryan's phone started buzzing away and the caller ID read, "Unknown."

Answering, Ryan simply said, "Price?"

"Yes detective it's me, your everyday nightmare. I have been trying to reach you detective but you wouldn't answer. Why is that, don't you care about the safety of Mrs. Metzger any longer?" Price's words were followed by severe coughing.

"Listen you mental case, if you harm that woman in any way I will cut your heart out personally and feed it to a dog."

Laughing, Price said, "We know it won't be your dog, don't we detective?"

"Look you son of a bitch….."

"No you look detective and listen close because I won't tell you this again. Every one of those drums of poison are booby trapped and if anyone even sneezes within five feet it with detonate. So my first advice to you and your band of idiots is to stay clear and don't attempt to move or spoil my plans. Is that clear, (cough, cough), detective?"

Hearing Price coughing once again caught Ryan's attention in a big way, so he asked, "What's the matter Price, has your little cold gotten worse? Sounds like you have a cough that needs attending too? Too bad your momma isn't around to tend to you?"

"Don't you (cough) ever talk about, (cough) my mother again, (cough) Ryan, (cough, cough)."

"Oh, did I hit a touchy spot in your heart Price?"

Obviously excited by Ryan's remarks about his mother Price said, "I can't wait (cough, cough) until I see you suffer Ryan, it will (cough, cough) give me great pleasure."

"Price, I'm yours for the taking, I'm ready for the exchange of me for Mrs. Metzger, where do we do it?"

"Do you think I'm stupid (cough, cough) detective?"

"No Price, actually I think you are a brilliant but psychotic sick individual whose brain should be left to science. So enough kissing up, let's get this trade underway. What are your demands for the exchange?"

"Detective, you will follow my (cough, cough) directions to the letter or (cough) your landlady will die at my (cough) hands personally, is that (cough, cough) understood?"

"You really need to do something about that cough Price. Yeah, understood I will be alone, now where?"

All the time Ryan had been on the phone with Price, Tyler had been on the phone with agents in her office who were running the operation of triangulating Price's location. As close as they could figure out, he was calling from a boat out on the ocean.

Tyler motioned to Ryan that they had a fix on Price and the Coast guard was being alerted. Ryan waved her off and mouthed the word, "No."

Ryan then said into his phone, "Okay Price no tricks, I'll be alone, but where?"

"You seemed to be so fond of the ocean detective, (cough) so this is what I want you to do with the help of that whore (cough) you have as a partner these days. I'm sure you are familiar with the Malibu Pier are you not?"

"Yeah go on."

"You will arrange to have that pier emptied of all people except yourself and Agent Tyler. You and the agent will climb down to the boat dock near the end of the pier and after your partner puts handcuffs on you behind your back in plain sight, she will leave. You will be watched every second so don't try any (cough, cough) heroics or this lovely lady at my side will get a bullet in her head, (cough) and be fed to the sharks. Is it all clear so far detective?"

"Yeah Price, its clear, go on."

"You will be picked up and your lady friend here will be left on the dock (cough) got that Ryan?"

"And when will all this take place Price?"

"It's 10AM now Ryan, I want you on that dock unarmed at (cough) noon, if you're not there she dies and I'll have to (cough, cough) wait for another day to kill you, still clear detective?"

"Price, the only problem……"

"NO PROBLEMS, just do it Ryan, I'll be watching, now get moving."

The line went dead and Ryan told Tyler, "We need to get moving and fast."

The FBI who had been monitoring the call contacted Ryan and told him they were on it. Agents were being sent to the pier to first evacuate everyone including business owners and their customers in the area.

Ryan would be wired with different transmitters for voice and location and have several keys for the cuffs hidden on his clothing. Since he would be unarmed he knew that his life would be at extreme risk and whatever plan he was concocting in his head would only have one shot of working.

Price had to know that he would be under constant surveillance from the time his boat first came into view and after the exchange was made. The money and manpower available to him made Price extremely dangerous. Like a cornered rat he always seemed to find a way to crawl through the smallest crack and escape leaving everyone watching with utter surprise.

With the Coast Guard posted at strategic locations out on the ocean, and the FBI snipers with their scoped rifles zeroed in on the drop-off spot, all they could do was sit and wait for Price to sail into the picture.

At 11:45 a high powered speed boat, the kind used by drug smugglers, appeared on the horizon and was headed at the exact compass reading as the Malibu Pier.

67

With Ryan and Tyler in position as instructed, in plain view of all the professional people involved, Tyler leaned over and kissed Ryan on the cheek and said, "Don't worry Hon we'll get the son of a bitch. We have people in the air and in the water so you'll be watched closely. All your tracking devices are working properly."

The cool ocean breeze was blowing through Ryan's hair and flapping his loosely fitting Hawaiian shirt as the speed boat got closer. Once the boat was at the small dock Ryan could see only a figure of a man in the cockpit and no one else. A second man appeared through a hatch holding

Dorothy Metzger by her arm as he led her to a small deck area at the stern of the boat.

Surprised that Price was actually keeping his word, Ryan yelled out over the sound of the engine noise, "Where's Price?"

Another man came through the hatchway, jumping onto the dock and grabbing Ryan, wrestling him on to the stern of the boat. With her hands tied in front of her Dorothy Metzger was pushed over the stern into the icy cold water as the boat turned and accelerated rapidly away from the dock.

Scrambling to save the woman's life the surrounding agents from out on Pacific Coast Highway rushed to the dock. By the time they arrived two divers who had been positioned submerged under the pier had already lifted the shivering woman to safety.

Ryan was gone and Mrs. Metzger was safe. So far everything was going as planned but now it was time for Ryan to make his escape. Problem was Price was not on the boat.

Reaching high speeds that the Coast Guard boats could not match, the speed boat headed north skimming over the ocean surface. Calls were made and additional Coast Guard boats were dispatched from northern locations. A Coast Guard helicopter high in the sky on silent running, kept the fleeing boat in constant view and reported any changes in direction.

Heading farther out to sea on course for the Anacapa Islands the question that was on everyone's mind was, "What is the next move that Price has in store and how does he plan to pull it off without being caught?"

With the boat getting closer to the islands the course it had taken was to the seaward side of the big island. The message that came in from the helicopter reported that there was an unusual amount of boat traffic in that area.

Approaching the dozen or so fishing boats the speed boat slowed its speed to a crawl as it nestled among the other drifting boats. Within minutes all of the other boats closed in on the speed boat and came so close on the calm seas that they were almost touching each other.

What followed was so very unpredictable that it caught the Coast Guard helicopter by surprise. Massive amounts of different colored smoke from what appeared to be smoke emitting machines engulfed the entire area making all the boats impossible to see. With orders for every one of the Coast Guard and FBI to keep away until the smoke had cleared they waited fifteen minutes for the first boat to be visible again.

Once the smoke had dissipated there was a blast from a loud foghorn and all of the boats took off in different directions. The speed boat that had been at the center with Ryan onboard had vanished.

When the reported disappearance of the speed boat came in, Tyler was the first to ask, "What the hell do you mean the boat disappeared, it couldn't just vanish in thin air?"

The agent on the Coast Guard helicopter repeated, "You heard me correctly Agent Tyler, it's gone, vanished."

The order was issued for all Coast Guard boats to stop, board and search all boats that were involved in the disappearance of Price's boat. There was a problem though, there were only six Coast Guard boats in the area along with the helicopter and the fleeing boats amounted to twelve. Since all of the twelve boats were moving at their top speed it would be hours until they were all located and searched.

Sitting in a small cove approximately a half mile from the action hidden by the rock formations of Anacapa Island, a thirty-two foot boat belonging the Dolphin Diving School was conducting diving exercises with what appeared to be a couple students. In reality they were all part of Price's master-planned getaway.

With all the boats leaving in such a rush and the area cleared out of all Coast Guard, a spotter high on the hilltop sent a signal to the little boat that all was clear.

Two divers were helped onto the stern of the boat and once their tanks and equipment were removed they proceeded to haul up something that was attached to a line hanging overboard. When the object broke the surface both men lifted it on board. Their prize now on board with them was a still handcuffed Det. Ryan complete with scuba tank and mask.

Once onboard, the other men in the elaborate getaway plot hid in the cabin and the anchor was hauled up. Slowly leaving the area, the boat headed for the Ventura Marina about fifteen miles away.

With the afternoon winds kicking in and the swells in the ocean slowing the speed of the boat, the trip would probably take forty-five minutes if all went well.

68

Sedated and covered with a canvas tarp as he lay on the stern deck of the little boat, Ryan could not tell where he was or where he was being taken. Whatever he had been injected with had him in a completely immobile state with only slight hearing and blurred sight.

As the boat engines idled down and men's voices could be heard giving instructions, a louder diesel engine could be heard and then bumping and rocking of the boat followed.

Ryan had no way of knowing that the boat was being loaded onto a trailer pulled by a large diesel powered truck that had backed down a boat ramp at a marina. With the sound of an electric winch pulling the boat onto the trailer on an extreme angle the next thing that followed was more voices and then the acceleration of the diesel engine.

Once again the sound of an engine idling was heard along with additional voices, and then they were on the move to somewhere. While the boat was traveling down the highway being hauled farther away from the marina, the Coast Guard was stopping and boarding all of the boats they could catch out on the ocean.

In each case the captain was placed under arrest and taken into custody for aiding a known criminal to escape from prosecution. Each captain had the same story and a copy of a contract from The Price Entertainment Co., "When we were contacted we were told that we were all being hired for a special effects spectacular that was being filmed for a TV special. We were all given a fifty-thousand dollar retainer with an additional fifty-thousand to follow if it all came off as planned."

When asked what had happened to the speed boat at the center of the grouping one of the captains said, "Hell, I couldn't believe it, they sunk the damn thing. That boat was equipped with some special plates on each side of the hull I guess that they removed and it went down like it was loaded with lead weights."

Not one of the captains questioned remembered seeing anyone get off the speed boat.

Two crewmen however remembered seeing scuba divers as the boat disappeared underwater.

With the new information about the scuba divers the site of the gathering of boats was revisited by the Coast Guard along with Agent Tyler on board. A floating buoy was found attached by a line to the sunken speed boat. On the buoy was what looked like an overnight bag and in the bag was Ryan's Hawaiian shirt and pants that appeared to have been ripped off of him and both his shoes. Tyler saw the contents and said, "Shit," as she picked up the two smashed mini transmitters that were lying in one of the shoes. The transmitter signals had stopped just before the boats all joined in a group.

When Tyler called her supervisor Chief Crane and gave her report she said, "There's still one transmitter they haven't found yet sir, but it has yet to be activated."

Tyler was instructed to return to the office to review the film tapes and everything they had on the botched capturing of Richard Price and the disappearance of Det. Ryan. By the time Tyler returned to the Federal Building she was immediately summoned to a conference room to view the tapes of the whole operation and a new discovery.

What she saw was a wide angle shot as the Coast Guard helicopter was circling the area over the back side of the island. One of the automatic cameras captured in its shot the bow of a small craft partially hidden by a rock formation that appeared anchored close to the cliffs.

Looking at earlier shots before the smoke screen had started; a much clearer shot of the boat had been recorded and was now in the lab hoping for enlargement and additional clarity.

By the time the enhanced picture was made available and a description was radioed to all the coastal marinas, six hours had passed since Ryan's disappearance but they now had a lead to follow. A call came back from the harbor master at the Ventura Marina. The man confirmed a boat fitting the description as being hauled out of the water about four hours earlier but had no additional information on the craft.

69

Still in a drugged state of mind, Ryan had been carried from the boat and locked in some type of storage shed. The key for the handcuffs that had been attached to a shoestring hanging around Ryan's neck had been cut off but the cuffs were still on his bloodied wrists.

As the fog in his mind seemed to clear and his eyes began to focus a little, Ryan tried to stand on his wobbly legs but fell to his knees quickly. Not knowing how much time had passed he could only try and concentrate on what had happened before he was drugged.

The men who had taken him from the dock were not familiar to him and he never saw Price on the boat. Time was moving very slowly and the sunlight that had been passing through the cracks in the dry wooden walls that surrounded him had disappeared. Every once in awhile there was a flash of light directed at the shed he appeared to be in, but other than that small bit of light, he was in total darkness. Trying to look through the small cracks to the outside was a useless effort.

With most of the drug effect almost gone Ryan heard voices speaking in Spanish as they got closer to his enclosure. In a loud burst of noise the door to the shack opened and two men walked in and grabbed him by his arms dragging him out onto the ground.

Standing in front of him draped in a dark colored poncho was Richard Price. Lifting his head slowly Ryan said in a graveled voice, "Glad you could join the party Price. Man you look like shit, how's that cough of yours, worse I hope?"

Price who appeared to have lost much weight since the last time Ryan saw him, had sunken and drawn in features in his face as he told the men in Spanish, "Bring him over (cough, cough) to the poles, I wish to hang him by his arms and watch him rot in the sun while the birds and rats eat at his flesh."

Ryan refusing to give his captor the satisfaction he desired, "Didn't I see this in an old pirate movie from the forties?"

"Make your jokes now Ryan, (Cough, cough), but you won't be joking very much longer."

Two poles that resembled fence posts were set in the ground about five feet apart and had shackle-rings that were above eye level. Set firmly in cement and positioned in front of an old barn, they looked like something that was constructed just for this occasion.

Again Price spoke in Spanish as he tossed the key for the handcuffs to one of the men and said, "Un-cuff him and tie him (cough, cough) to the posts."

Hanging by his bruised and bloody wrists that had been severely cut by the handcuffs, Ryan slowly lifted his head and said, "You need to do something about that cough Price, you wouldn't want to kick off before me, would you, and spoil your fun?"

Walking slowly up to the hanging defenseless detective, Price stood about two feet away and spit in Ryan's face and said, "Here, have some of the poison that's killing me."

With all he could muster, Ryan smiled and said, "I knew there had to be some reward in all of this. You're dying from your own medicine?"

With no answer from his captor, the scowl on Price's face was all the reward Ryan needed at that moment but he knew he couldn't last much longer hanging there.

Sixty miles to the south an excited FBI agent, who had been monitoring and waiting for a signal from Ryan's last transmitter, rushed into the conference room and said, "I got him! He's up in the Ventura area. I have his exact location pinpointed with the coordinates"

Within minutes two helicopters loaded with FBI agents were lifting off and headed for the Ventura location. Agents from the Ventura area were instructed to slowly take up positions in the outlying areas of the location and keep a low profile.

70

Price, who was well equipped at his location had one of his men constantly listening in on all radio bands including the digital bands used by the police departments and the FBI. With complete radio silence instructions being observed all communications were being handled by cell phones only.

The location of the property where Ryan was being held captive was part of a huge orange grove nestled in the foothills in a very remote area of Ventura. With nothing but adjoining orange grove ranches with a clear view of the valley to the west and mountains to the east, helicopters coming into the area would be spotted immediately.

The plan that had been thrown together in the urgency of the rescue operation included landing at the local airport and traveling by car to the location. Several of the agents involved had sniper training and were equipped with the weapons to overpower and seize the property when and if necessary.

On the command of the senior special agent in charge, Agent Charles Blake, agents who had completely surrounded the area started to move in but were instructed not to make any contact.

Two agents who were both ex Navy Seals familiar with rescue operations, worked their way in through the orange groves dressed like migrant workers in case they were spotted. Both men were of Spanish descent and spoke the language fluently and could plead that they were only looking for work if they were caught on the property.

Equipped with cell phones, pocket knives and one small caliber automatic weapon, each of the men as they cleared the groves spotted what appeared to be a man hanging between two posts. Being careful not to be seen, the men dropped back into the orange grove and one of them called in a quick report describing Ryan's situation and how he appeared unconscious or dead.

Their instructions were to stay where they were and keep out of sight, but it was too late. They had been spotted by one of Price's men who were approaching them. Rather than try to hide or run, the one agent waved and said to the approaching man in Spanish, "Amigo, we're looking for work, any kind of work."

Price's man who was carrying a rifle, turned to point at the house and said, "The owner who lives in the big house does not need anymore help around here." Those were the last words the man would ever speak as one of the agents quickly put one hand over the man's mouth and with the other sliced his throat.

Dragging the man deeper into the grove the agent called his superior and reported the action that had been taken. By this time several more agents had gotten themselves into better positions around the property but unfortunately were spotted by a couple of Price's men.

Under the watchful eyes of several agents the two men ran from the grove towards Ryan who never even raised his head until he heard shots and watched as both agents hit the ground. Trying to clear his throat and yell as loud as he could, Ryan yelled out, "No, you bastard, no."

Although both agents wore Kevlar vests under their shirts, one of them had been shot in the face, but the other was only stunned by several shots striking him in the chest, knocking the wind out of him.

Agents by this time were firing at men who were positioned at the side of the barn and at the second floor of the ranch house where shots were coming from.

Price, who had also been at the side of the barn talking with a couple of his men, somehow worked his way through the barn and came out in a direct line behind Ryan. In fear of hitting Ryan no one could shoot at Price.

Running up behind Ryan coughing uncontrollably, Price held a pitchfork in his hands and yelled out, "It's now your turn to die Ryan (cough, cough) it can't wait any longer. I've waited for this moment for a long time."

Price missed his opportunity as the pitch fork fell to the ground after a shot from the left side of the yard struck him in his left shoulder.

Knocked backward for an instant, Price lifted his poncho and removed a hunting knife from its sheath on his belt and slowly continued towards Ryan once again, coughing as he hobbled.

A second shot fired from the right side of the yard struck Price in his knee shattering it and dropping him to the ground on top of the pitch fork.

Rising to his feet again picking up the pitch fork, Price made one last attempt to charge at Ryan with the weapon pointed straight ahead.

Running towards Price from the side, Agent Tyler fired several shots at his head splattering skull fragments and brain matter on Ryan but it was a nasty shower Ryan enjoyed.

With their leader lying dead, the remainder of Price's men threw down their weapons and surrendered.

Once the area was proclaimed safe and secure, emergency vehicles swarmed onto the property attending to the wounded and recording the names of the dead where possible. Ryan had been cut down from the hanging posts and was loaded into an ambulance but said, "I refuse to leave without Agent Tyler, get her here now."

When the ambulance door opened up again Ryan asked, "What took you so long sweetheart?"

Sitting down next to Ryan as the doors closed behind her she said, "We didn't get the signal until the cuffs came off."

Ryan asked, "What are you talking about?"

"When the key got inserted into the handcuffs it sent out a transmitter signal and we were able to zero in on your location."

"Don't you think it would have been a good idea to let me know about another one of your toys?"

"There wasn't time Ryan. By the time I asked if you knew, you were already on that boat. By the way, how was your diving experience?"

"With the shit they injected into me I thought it was all a dream. By the time I started coming to and saw my shirt and pants were gone and my shorts were wet, I thought I just pissed in my pants from the excitement. You know something sweetheart, Price was dying and he knew it. The bastard was dying from his own medicine."

Tyler said, "That's funny, the dead man's own medicine was killing him. I wonder how that happened to such an intelligent man."

"Maybe his own people fed it to him?"

"I wouldn't put it past them, all considering."

Laughing, Ryan said, "They say high cholesterol kills, don't you know that?"

"Yeah, but it wasn't soon enough."

The paramedic said, "I think that's about it for now, he needs to get some rest agent."

Ryan said, "Wait, one more thing sweetheart. What about all that poison Price had booby-trapped at the reservoirs?"

"It was all a hoax, the drums were there okay, but they were filled with colored water and nothing but road flares, batteries and alarm clocks wired to them. We did find a few gallons of that poison in a secret compartment at his Calabasas home, but nothing more."

Ryan motioned for Tyler to bend down a little closer so he could whisper in her ear and said, "You got anymore of those bureau gadgets in your bag of tricks that we could use after I'm patched up and ready for a little affection from my favorite agent?"

Kissing him on the cheek Tyler said, "I got something that has batteries that the bureau knows nothing about. It will be in my bag of tricks when you and I finally get to that Las Vegas vacation you promised me.

THE END

THE END